Where Tulips Bloom

Journey Publishers
Mt. Pleasant, Michigan

Where Tulips Bloom
Copyright © 2007 by Patricia Palmer Benson
All rights reserved.

Except as permitted under United States Copyright Law, no part of this publication may be reproduced or distributed in any form or by any means, or stored in a database or retrieval system, without the prior written permission of the publisher.

First Edition
December 2007

Written by:
Patricia Jane Palmer
With
Sarah R. Adams

Cover design and formatting by:
Lori Block

Book printing by:
Gorham Printing
Centralia, Washington

General Counsel:
Jeffrey J. Palmer

Published in the United State of America
By
Journey Publishers, LLC
Mt. Pleasant, Michigan

JourneyPublishers.com

To Jeff, Matt, Randy, and Kevin.
A Legacy of Love.

– Patricia Jane Palmer

To my family for their constant love and support:
My parents, Roger and Joann,
and Andrea, Jon, Rachel and Abby

And to Peter . . .

– Sarah R. Adams

Where Tulips Bloom

WhereTulipsBloom.com

CHAPTER ONE
When Tulips Bloom

I grew up believing I was ordinary. In fact, I grew up believing that life itself, with all of its facets of family and the confines of our small Michigan community was, in fact, ordinary.

But every once in a while, in an ordinary life, love gives you a fairytale. And this is the story of mine.

As most little girls, I grew up wishing and hoping for my very own Prince Charming—the "one" who would make all of my dreams come true—and, like any real-life Cinderella, my ordinary life as a girl growing up on a farm would be transformed into one of a fairytale princess . . . It's funny when things turn out even better than you could've ever wished . . .

"Mom?"

"Mom, did you hear what I said?"

Her son's voice suddenly pulled Pat Oswald Palmer to the present where she sat across the café table from him. She smiled at him and nodded, scolding herself for allowing her thoughts to drift away for a moment.

"Of *course,* I heard what you said, Jeff," she said reassuringly, trying to refocus.

Jeff shook his head with a knowing smile. He knew her too well for that.

"Nice try, Mom. You were somewhere else just now. Are you all right?"

Pat laughed, took another sip of the steaming tea in front of her, and attempted to change the subject back to her eldest son's on-going conversation about something he'd read in his beloved *Wall Street Journal*. She loved hearing about his ambitions, loved encouraging his tendency to dream big—but today . . . today, it seemed that other things were occupying her thoughts . . . other places . . . other people . . . other times . . .

Every once in a while, in an ordinary life, love gives you a fairytale . . .

It was a phrase that echoed in my mind on days like today, a beautiful song from the past, taking me somewhere far, far away. The warm sunshine brought back echoes of distant laughter, the dazzling blue sky seemed to carry a familiar, almost-forgotten melody, the warm breeze stirred memories of romance and love . . . Today was a good day for remembering . . .

It was a beautiful day in downtown Mt. Pleasant, Michigan—the perfect afternoon for a quick lunch with her son, Jeff, at their favorite downtown café before she steered her minivan onto the freeway for an afternoon on the road for work. Pat loved that about her job, that it gave her the freedom to keep up the ever-important balance of work and family. Those two aspects of her life had always brought her great joy. In fact, she had always said that every part of her life made her happy—just as it had for a long, long time.

Today, a brilliant sun had been shining when she had left her office at Central Michigan University to head downtown to meet Jeff. While it had officially been spring for nearly two months, it was only now, in early May, that the signs of spring had begun to reveal themselves—almost seemingly reluctantly—to Michigan.

It had been a particularly brutal Midwestern winter, stretching from a bone-chilling Thanksgiving on through to a wintry Easter Sunday. But winter, as Pat knew all too well, never lasts forever, and today—ah, today, weathermen were, at long-last, forecasting sunny skies and seventy degrees—the true sign that spring had finally arrived.

Today was, Pat had thought as she left her office, the perfect day to be traveling to the Flint area to conduct a school seminar. As she had loaded the last of her materials—the usual piles of teacher packets, handouts, and an office kit of essentials—into her minivan, she had glanced at her watch and brightened, realizing that she had just enough time to drive by her favorite sight of Michigan springtime. Pat had smiled as she began the route that she knew would take her past her favorite tulip garden.

Mt. Pleasant lived up to its name, a *pleasant* community comprised of college students, faculty, business people, farmers, storeowners, and families whose generational ties to the area went as far back as anyone could remember.

Mt. Pleasant was home to Central Michigan University—where Pat had attended college, and locals had, in the past, harbored a love-hate relationship with the 20,000 college students who descended onto the sleepy community each Fall. But times were changing, and their town was growing rapidly as new stores, restaurants, apartment complexes, and office buildings sprung up where corn stalks and grains had once waved against the sky.

Even with the changing landscape, Pat had always loved May and the garden of tulips in front of CMU's Wightman Hall, lovingly tended by the University's groundskeepers for as long as anyone could remember. Pat slowed her car to admire the early-blooming reds and yellows that were now fully open and waving gently in the warm spring breeze.

Tulips, she mused, are *just like the pennants announcing grand openings and new beginnings . . .*

The brightly-colored tulips had always fascinated her. There was something oddly-comforting in the fact that they provided continuity and consistency, returning each year to the grounds of Wightman Hall—and yet they also simultaneously symbolized new birth, new beginnings, fresh starts, and heralded the arrival of spring.

They are just like life, she had found herself thinking, almost wistfully. *A balance of the mundane and normalcy mingled with new twists and turns—just enough to keep a person conscious and curious about the future . . .*

Tulips were a perfect metaphor for the complexities of life. But, in truth, they also simply made Pat Palmer happy.
The gardens at Wightman Hall had been in place for years, which had perhaps spurred on the nostalgic mood she found herself immersed in now as she and Jeff sat chatting over lunch. She remembered admiring the tulips decades ago when she had been an undergraduate student at Central Michigan University, who spent a lot of time in Wightman Hall.

It seems so, so long ago—and yet it was only yesterday that tulips were blooming and my life was in transition, caught between childhood and adulthood . . .

Midway through her fifth decade, it seemed ironic and almost poetic that it might be the same bulbs still blooming after all these long winters had passed. Pat had made a mental note to ask her second oldest son, a landscape designer, if this could be true. Do tulip bulbs bloom for thirty-some years? Does *anything* really bloom for that long?
Pat smiled, knowing that it did.

Every once in a while, in an ordinary life, love gives you a fairytale . . .

Pulled back to the present once more, Pat was aware of the busy café around her, the clanging of silverware, and the smell of fresh coffee. She and Jeff had agreed earlier that morning to meet at the downtown sandwich shop where they sat now. *Stan's*, she recalled, had been a part of Mt. Pleasant for as long as the tulips.

The small, no-frills place had been in business since the 1960's. The booths were dated and chairs worn from years of college students gathering to study, eat sandwiches, and consume gallons of caffeine during exam time.

The tables were decorated with worn plastic flowers, but the homemade soups and sandwiches kept the locals coming back decade after decade. It was a favorite meeting spot for area business owners and professionals to discuss local issues over morning coffee.

As she took in the room, Pat caught a glimpse of her own reflection in a nearby window, smiling and nodding along to Jeff's dialogue. Many years ago, her reaction to her reflection had been one of indifference, but those who knew her now described her in terms that she had come to accept. One of Jeff's friends had once said that she balanced lightness and laughter with depth and perception. She was feminine and soft and, simultaneously, a strong leader, possessing both convictions and passion. Pat felt satisfied with that description. It wasn't too many years earlier that she was certain she would have been described in other terms: shy, quiet, timid . . . a true wallflower . . .

It's funny how things can change so, so much . . .

Pat turned her attention back to Jeff, studying his face as she often did with each of her sons. The midday sun poured through the window near the booth where they sat, and she squinted against it, but her eyes never left Jeff's face.

Remarkable, she thought, *how much he looks like Jim . . .*

Pat always welcomed the chance to lunch with Jeff. As her children became adults—Jeff was now in his early thirties—she considered it an honor and a privilege to be included in their lives.

He had from the day he was born, looked very much indeed like Jim with his sandy-colored hair, blue-green eyes, and fair skin. At 5′ 11,″ he was just a little shorter than his dad. His mannerisms, too, she noted, matched Jim's. Jeff sat with his index finger extended, his chin resting on his folded fingers and thumb—his hands were also replicas of Jim's.

Jeff continued talking, his voice smooth, both gentle and forceful at the same time. Pat's friends often said that Jeff could call them any time, they loved the sound of his voice.

Then, Pat guiltily realized that she wasn't listening to her son again and attempted to focus on the conversation once more.

"So, ultimately, people will rise up because within the human spirit there will always be a yearning to be free. It is a basic need for all people" Jeff was saying in earnest. "I mean, what are this country's leaders thinking? That we will trade our freedom for a false sense of security?"

He laughed, shaking his head in disbelief at his rhetorical question.

Pat smiled affectionately at him. She loved her son's laugh.
Almost a masculine giggle.

Jeff was neatly dressed in a business-casual, freshly-pressed blue shirt with grey dress slacks and cordovan wingtips, completing his usual conservative professional look. She guessed that he must have been meeting with a client that afternoon. Her son was an estate planning attorney with his own fledging practice in Mt. Pleasant.

Pat felt a surge of pride, as she always did, when she thought of Jeff's choice to focus his efforts on helping people realize their dreams and legally plan for passing on legacies of their values and beliefs. It was a struggle to build a clientele in the estate planning area of law. Unlike divorces and bankruptcies, Jeff dealt with issues that seemed to have little urgency and were often pushed aside until some time in the future.

Pat and Jim had always tried to instill in their children that the time to think about the future was the present, and Jeff followed their advice to the letter and passed it along to his clients. It was something he felt very, very strongly about.

The study of law was perfectly suited to Jeff.

"Mom, if they designed a course of study absolutely perfectly suited for me, it would be law!"

She could still hear his passionate words echoing in her head when he declared his intent to become a lawyer. She had been delighted, knowing her son had indeed found his passion and a field perfect for him. Pat knew all too well that it is too rare in life that people discover their passion in life and manage to fashion that into a career.

Pat smiled again with satisfaction that her eldest was happy and content in pursuing his dreams. She had, herself, always been one to pursue what she wanted.

Jeff, as oldest children often are, was bright and mature—a visionary. His intelligence and ability to see the 'big picture' could hardly be compared to many in the general public. He was loved deeply and considered a blessing, as were all of the Palmer boys, although Jeff had *certainly* been a handful as a child.

Pat was certain that when James Dobson wrote the book, <u>The Strong-Willed Child</u>, he had used her son, Jeff, as his prime example. His stubbornness came in handy in the courtroom, though. Pat's sister Suezell had frequently joked that if they all had known when Jeff was a toddler that his adamant stance was just preparation for being an attorney, it would have been easier to tolerate his tantrums.

Of course, Jeff's most unique quirk, Pat reflected, was his strong opinions regarding *everything*. Jeff would often argue firmly-held beliefs with anyone until he convinced the other party that he was simply *right* and that they were simply *wrong*.

But, strong opinions and stubbornness included, Jeff was a good, caring person who was particularly supportive and protective of those closest to him, particularly his younger brother, Randy. Now nearly twenty-seven, Randy still turned to Jeff for advice from time to time.

Perhaps because of his extraordinary abilities, life had not always been as easy for Jeff as Pat wished. He often had a different perspective on life than those around him. He was sociable yet shy, and Pat wasn't certain he was always comfortable in his own skin. It was an observation that made her yearn for ways to smooth life's road for him. He had so much to offer, and she dearly hoped that he truly believed that about himself, too.

Their conversation turned to Jeff's involvement in the local crisis pregnancy center and the church where he served as a trustee. Pat knew that it all kept her eldest son busy; but she knew he also reserved time for his close-knit group of friends who served as a sort of second family for him.

"How are your friends doing these days?" Pat asked, breathing a prayer of gratitude for their presence in his life. They were a great group of "kids," all from different walks of life and in their twenties and thirties, who had connected at Jeff's church and lived their lives together, spending free time barbecuing, going to movies, even just sitting around, talking and being together.

"They are all doing well," Jeff replied, taking a sip of his coffee. "Chuck and Jules are still in their Honeymoon phase—even after being married almost a year. They've started a new tradition of having everyone over for lunch after church every Sunday afternoon. It'll save us all some money. Eating out every Sunday was getting expensive!"

Pat smiled. Jeff often remarked that Chuck and Julie Pepper's love story reminded him of his parents' romance of true love.

"What about Sarah and Andrea? How are they doing?" Pat prompted, always curious about the two sister-like roommates with whom her son spent much of his time. Their antics and closeness reminded Pat so much of her and her lifelong best friend, Debbie.

"Well, Andrea just brought home a new puppy," Jeff replied with a chuckle. "And Sarah was *really not* happy about it, but those two are inseparable; they'll get it figured out. Besides, Sarah is spending most of her time traveling for work these days. She works way too much."

Pat smiled.

"Are she and Andrea still your 'dates' for the wedding?"

Jeff laughed.

"That's the plan," he responded in amusement. "And, Mom, I know what you're thinking: they are both *just* friends, so don't get any ideas, okay?"

Pat laughed and threw her hands up in defeat.

"Oh, all right," she conceded with a smile, taking another sip of her tea.

Pat was sincerely grateful that Jeff had friends like the two of them, though. His life was a full one, if not always an easy one. She did, however, not-so-secretly wish that Jeff would find the love of his life.

Pat took great satisfaction in the fact that she was known for her success in matchmaking and often wondered if she might some day provide some help in this endeavor with Jeff. She had, after all, helped her son, Matt, meet the girl who was now his wife of three years.

Pat was a hopeless romantic and personally held to the belief that love was the ultimate goal in life. Jeff, however, often seemed more closed-off to emotion than Matt. Some days, it seemed that there were still scars visible in Jeff that spoke of losses in the past.

All the more reason to find love, Pat had often said. *It has a transformational power unlike anything else.*

It was something she herself knew all too well . . .

Every once in a while, in an ordinary life, love gives you a fairytale . . .

"Speaking of the wedding," Jeff interrupted her thoughts. "Have you talked to Kevin this week? How are the plans coming along?"

Pat and the whole Palmer family were happily anticipating a family wedding that summer. Kevin, the youngest of her sons, in contrast to Jeff, had always seemed to take life in stride, including his upcoming marriage. Andrea, whom he had met in college, was a wonderful young woman They had been engaged since the day after their graduation nearly one year ago.

"Well," Pat replied. "Things are rolling along. I went with Andrea last week to pick out her dress—it's absolutely beautiful! And I thought it was so sweet of her to invite me along."

"That was really thoughtful," Jeff agreed. "I know you must be wishing you had a daughter after helping to plan so many weddings."

Pat smiled. There was a time when all she wanted in the world was a daughter of her own. But God had other plans and, now, she couldn't imagine a life without four unique and wonderful sons.

Pat was thankful that Kevin and Andrea had each found local positions in engineering and teaching, respectively. The economy in Michigan had forced many young people to leave the area to seek employment, and she was more than a little thankful that Kevin and Andrea would be close by.

The conversation between Pat and Jeff then switched to her role as director of Michigan Schools in the Middle. Jeff asked about her upcoming seminar that afternoon. There were eighteen middle schools engaged in school improvement and their leadership teams would be coming together to network and continue their work. She would be part of a team of facilitators who would lead the professional development session. Sometimes it seemed surreal that she was director of a nationally-recognized center that had been successful in helping many young adolescents from low-income backgrounds become well-educated, caring, and productive members of their communities. She loved her work and took little credit for its success. She had been very fortunate to hire some of the best professional development coaches in the field. Pat believed that it was her job to support and provide training opportunities for those whom she led.

Pat glanced at her watch and knew that she must get on the road to make it to her facilitators meeting by late afternoon. She picked up the check—it was a small way to help support Jeff financially. She was glad that he was doing what he loved. She, herself, would have probably felt compelled to accept an offer from a firm with a guaranteed salary and benefits, but Jeff was brave, and blessed—or cursed—with more than a small dose of independence. She said goodbye to Jeff and he, as always, thanked her for lunch.

Pat dreaded driving to schools—it was mostly the schools in urban areas that made her nervous. She was easily lost and had always felt a little insecure about her ability to drive in the city. It was, she recalled, one of the things that her staff had gotten used to—her calling on her cell phone asking them to get on Mapquest to help her find a school.

Bless them, she thought, *what would I do without them?*

Today, with the sunshine brightening the drive, Pat didn't mind the two hour trip ahead of her.

So she pulled out on Mount Pleasant's Mission Street and headed south to catch US-127. Mid-week traffic was mild so the drive promised to be relaxing and pleasant.

Every once in a while, in an ordinary life, love gives you a fairytale . . .

Perhaps because she had just finished lunch with Jeff, or it could have been talking about Kevin's upcoming wedding. Or maybe it was because of the spring tulips. Whatever the reason, she allowed herself to mentally travel back in time. It was something she did not often let herself do . . . too many memories, too intense And her Mother's advice often echoed in her ears reminding her, *"There is nothing we can do about it, so don't think about it."*

This advice usually left her squarely in the present, which wasn't a bad place to be, just very, very different from another life she had known.

But today . . . Today was a good day for remembering . . . And so it was, once again, years earlier in a small but growing community in Mid-Michigan, where a fairytale began and changed her life forever . . .

Chapter Two
Happy Days

Every story has a beginning. Mine begins in the usual way: a hospital, my mother, nurses and doctors, hopes, dreams and prayers already being invested in the new life about to be born . . . I can't know exactly what my mother was thinking and feeling as I entered the world, but even then, I knew I was surrounded by love . . .

It was the happiest day of Naomi Oswald's life, she was sure of it. And in spite of numerous doses of painkillers surrounding her brain in a pleasant dreamy fog, she found herself telling anyone within earshot, "I have a baby girl! I have a baby girl!"

Little Patricia Jane Oswald was born September 12, 1950, with bright sparkling eyes and a healthy set of lungs. It was what might've been the most beautiful late summer afternoon, her birth temporarily interrupting the family's annual navy bean harvest. It was just three days before her mother's birthday, which Naomi insisted was a perfect gift from her newborn daughter.

Romaine and Naomi, Pat's parents, had been a typical couple of the era, falling in love in spite of a World War exploding around them, Romaine had served almost four years overseas before he was finally discharged from the Army and allowed to return home to his love. The couple married in 1945.

Their first son, Tom, was born seventeen months after they were married and Victor followed just fifteen months later. Little Pat was delighted with the arrival of her sister, Suezell, born four years after her. Suezell's birth would be one of the greatest joys in Pat's young life. The two little girls had a relationship that parents wish for their daughters. Pat could scarcely remember a fight during their childhood years. Suezell had become her best friend, one of those who grows and changes with you and remains your closest confidant for life. The seeds of childlike closeness and sharing had blossomed into a close bond as adults.

Pat and Suezell's childhood days were golden, filled with dolls, "playing house," and traveling to any magical place their imaginations would take them. Both girls loved dressing up their dolls for doll shows, presented to their parents—an audience held hostage by their adorable little girls. Stealing all the family shoes to play shoe store was another favorite pastime, along with dressing the family cats in doll clothes and putting them to bed in the dolls' beds.

Summers seemed like magic, long warm days of endless glasses of lemonade and playing in the backyard. One summer, the inventive duo put on their very own dance recital by performing in their swimsuits on a picnic table for Grandma and Grandpa. The two young beauties were convinced that their path in life was definitely leading to the runways of Paris!

Summer was shrouded in a dreamlike fog, with snapshot memories of riding "horses" around the yard—in reality, they were yard rakes—and performing circus-worthy feats on the rope that swung freely in the barn.

Pat and Suezell, as do most little girls, endlessly dreamed, imagined and acted out their wedding days—an old lace curtain becoming an elegant bridal gown and lots of snowball flowers and tulips in the yard to throw as bouquets.

"Pat," a wide-eyed Suezell whispered, one sunny afternoon during one such wedding. "Will you come to my wedding some day?"

"Of course," Pat replied. "And you'll come to my wedding, too."

"You're going to get married, too?" Suezell asked, as if the thought of her big sister's future had escaped her young imagination.

Pat's eyes sparkled. "Yes, I am!" she said decidedly. "I'm going to marry a very handsome boy, and I'm going to wear a long white dress with pink flowers and lace."

Little Suezell suddenly looked worried. "But then you'll move away, won't you? That will make me cry, Pat."

Pat threw little girl arms around her sister. "We will always be best friends, though, no matter what. I promise."

Summer also gave the children time and opportunity to attend every Vacation Bible School the two girls could find. The church-sponsored events helped to break up the long summers, and rescued the children from the bean fields where they were expected to help with the hoeing. Hot, sweaty, bumblebee-filled afternoons in the bean field became the setting for Pat's vow to get a good education in order to avoid hoeing beans for a living! Eventually, she gladly traded baking rolls, cookies, pies and inside chores for messy outdoor work.

Early adolescence found Pat totally unprepared for life beyond a childhood that had been carefree and filled with good times. It simply seemed to catch her off guard . . .

"What's wrong?" Suezell's little forehead wrinkled in a worried crease at the sight of her sister's frown.

Pat threw her schoolbag down onto the floor and silently slid onto a chair, helping herself to some of her mother's fresh cookies and avoiding eye contact with her little sister.

"Pat, why are you sad?" Suezell persisted, her face growing more anxious.

"I don't understand boys," Pat mumbled, staring at the cookie in her hands.

"Boys? Understand, what?" Suezell asked in confusion.

"You wouldn't understand, Suezell," Pat said with a sigh.

It had been a truly awful and confusing day. What had started as an ordinary morning for an ordinary sixth grader had turned into a nightmare. Even now, sitting across the kitchen table from Suezell, the memory replayed in her head with painful clarity.

"Pat," a whisper had hissed from the next row of neatly-lined desks.

Pat looked up, startled from her absorption in her studies. It was Joe, the boy in the next row, with sandy blonde hair and ears that pointed strangely in some direction that Pat was sure defied gravity.

Pat nervously glanced at their teacher at the front of the room, fearing repercussions from talking in class, but Mrs. Grice was intently grading papers and busily scratching out lesson plans for the following day while her students worked quietly.

"Pssst, Pat," Joe repeated, more insistently this time.

Pat had forced herself to meet his gaze, before saying "What, Joe?" in a barely-audible voice.

"I like you."

Color stained Pat's cheeks, and she sharply drew in a breath. What on Earth was she supposed to say? She hadn't even considered a 'boyfriend' type of relationship. The moment seemed to freeze in time as poor Joe stared expectantly at her. Pat merely buried her head in her grammar book and never spoke to Joe again.

Boys are dumb! She found herself repeating again and again in her mind, in an almost assuring manner as she continued to nibble cookies in the safety of her own kitchen. As Suezell changed the subject from her big sister's woes to her own afternoon of playtime, Pat promised herself that boys wouldn't ever make her feel that way again. The awful afternoon was behind her, and she would never again find herself in that situation.

Pat became painfully shy around all boys, from that moment right through graduation from high school, but her shyness did not extend to her schoolwork and extra-curricular activities. She was always willing to give speeches in the classroom, and she didn't have any trouble talking to other girls—in retrospect with years and years as a teacher behind her, she often wondered if her own teachers didn't wish she was less chatty.

Without even realizing it, Jim and I were growing up, only miles from one another, in what some might call a perfect world that revolved around solid values, family, friends, and learning how to be a good neighbor. Our families were very different, of course, but I think we both always treasured the protected universe that was the haven for our childhood days . . .

In so many ways, Jim was growing up in *Andy Griffith's* "Mayberry," set on acres and acres of woods and farmland in Mid-Michigan. It was the Golden Era of the 1950's, and the pace of life always seemed slower on the cozy Palmer farm than in other places: winters were warm beneath hand-made quilts, summer afternoons were golden and bright, and neighbors always had time to stop and visit over coffee or iced tea in rocking chairs on the porch.

The Palmers were a typical farm family from that era in time, with little Jim growing up the middle child of a family of five. Jim's father, Leslie, a bright, hard-working family man, maintained a small cash crop and dairy farm that included the usual Midwestern assortment of navy beans, corn, wheat, alfalfa for hay and some oats. Each night at suppertime, Jim's mother, Ida Mae, was dressed in an apron, presenting lavish meat-and-potato meals. Everyone did what he or she was "supposed" to do by virtue of God, family and the all-American creed: work hard, be honest, and live by "The Golden Rule."

Ida Mae, was a quintessential 1950's Mom, delighting in

dazzling her family and neighbors with homemade bread, pies, and cookies; she peeled potatoes at lightning speed, and cooked a roast beef that seemed to melt in the mouths of hungry guests. Ida Mae Palmer was known throughout the neighborhood as the "county's best cook," and the woman whose table was always filled to overflowing with "Blue Ribbon" quality comfort foods for anyone who stopped by. She loved every opportunity to feed hardworking neighbor farmers and their families.

Jim, by any standards, was an easy child, born the day after Christmas in 1948, Ida Mae's pride and joy and the perfect Christmas gift for the Palmer family. He was every parent's dream in so many respects, the child who voluntarily went to bed when he grew tired, even as a toddler. He was very shy, quiet and well-behaved, the son who never gave his parents a day of worry. Doing the right thing seemed to come easily to Jim, and his mother always smiled at his obedience and overall good nature, admiring the quiet determination that showed itself, even at a young age.

"Jimmy? Is that you?"

The kitchen screen door squeaked a bit on its hinges, a sound that Ida Mae had come to love. She secretly hoped her husband would never think to grease the hinges: with each creak, another member of her family announced that he or she had returned to the safety of hearth and home—just the way Ida Mae preferred it. On this particular afternoon, she smiled in anticipation as her little Jimmy appeared in the doorway, home from his first day of kindergarten.

She smiled warmly at him, abandoning the ironing and hurrying to get him a snack.

"Hi, Jimmy!"

"Hi, Mother," he replied solemnly, apparently lost in thought as he quietly placed his bag on the floor and climbed onto a chair.

"Well, how did it go?" she inquired, placing a glass of milk and a fresh, warm muffin in front of him.

Jimmy was quiet for a moment, as if in deep reflection. He took a bite of his snack and met his mother's gaze in determination.

"Well, if I don't learn anything more tomorrow than I did today, I'm not going back!"

Ida Mae suppressed an amused smile as she attempted to explain to her son that he would indeed learn much, much more as time passed.

Time did indeed pass, albeit slowly, on the Palmer farm. The homestead had, as many others that dotted the Michigan countryside, a red hip-roof barn, green-shingled roof and fenced barnyard for the dairy cows. The two-acre site provided ample areas of grass for the collie dog, Laddie, to run and play with energetic boys. Change came slowly to this pastoral setting. Even the family's series of collies maintained the same name—Laddie— over and over again.

The lawn surrounding the house and outbuildings was always freshly mowed and what pink magic petunias their limited budget could afford, were carefully maintained as a source of pride for Ida Mae. The yard also included deep purple lilacs, tulips in assorted reds and yellows, a white spirea bush, towering hollyhocks, pink and white peonies, and vibrant yellow roses that bloomed throughout the summer. The yard was also home to an assortment of cats—kept plump with warm, creamy milk from the cows and comforted from chilly nights in the golden straw mows in the barn. What the small, white wood-frame house lacked in amenities was made up for in its cleanliness shrouded in constant mouth-watering aroma of fresh baked goods.

The house, grounds and buildings, in so many ways, seemed a tribute to the family and to the era itself—it was functional and simply met the needs of the family. In the winter, the yard was filled with sleds and snowmen fashioned by little boys hands. Boys who hurried inside the house after hours of play in the cold would warm their hands and feet by the space heater and eat homemade cookies, fresh and warm from a wood-burning cook stove.

Jimmy was, on all counts, an adorable little boy with sandy-colored hair and freckles sprinkled across his face; his ears were slightly bigger than some would wish for, but still he glowed with the spark of being wholesome and healthy, a child with all-American good looks.

His parents were pleased with their son in so many ways: he was mature beyond his years, willingly completing his chores in the barn and in the field when asked.

During the day, Jim attended a one-room country school about a mile from his home. Kindergarten through eighth grades learned from one teacher who challenged two dozen farm kids to learn their 3 R's. Recesses included baseball games and fun on the swings and slide, and lunchboxes were filled with sandwiches, fruit, and homemade cookies. Like many of his friends, Jim walked to and from school with his older brother, Richard, and younger brother, Ted. Although nearly eight years separated them, Jim was close to his brother, Ted, and he would frequently do chores for him that Ted preferred not to do.

Jim Palmer was in eighth grade when all the area country schools closed and students were bussed into St. Louis Public Schools. This had meant real change for him, too, it was a trying ordeal going from a school with 25 neighbor kids to attending a "town" school with 125 students per grade. For a somewhat-shy young adolescent like Jim, life was suddenly about adjusting to a new environment, meeting new students, and navigating unfamiliar hallways.

It was the same year that he and the whole Palmer family had moved to another farm about five miles away from his childhood home. The house was a large, Victorian-style home with a big wrap-around porch shaded by large lilac bushes and spirea shrubs. It had more of life's luxuries, and the family, enjoyed television in the evenings and cartoons on Saturday morning in the winter months.

"Teddy, can ya hand me that empty bucket?"

Young Jim Palmer stood up and stretched his back, slightly stiffened, after stooping over to pick green beans in his mother's garden for the past two hours. Jim smiled, letting the late summer sun ease the knots in his shoulders, as his younger brother appeared among the plants, bucket in hand.

"Here ya go, Jimmy," Teddy said, a weary frown creasing his forehead, "How much longer do we have to do this?"

Jim smiled again in amusement as Ted sighed, moving back to his area of picking on the other side of the spacious garden plot. Jim himself didn't mind chores like this. To him, farm work was good work: predictable and solid, operating under rules that stayed the same and seasons that rotated with consistency. Ted, on the other hand, had mentioned on more than one occasion that he'd much rather be riding his bicycle or playing baseball than working in the garden. Most of Jim's friends agreed with Ted's preference to be doing anything but chores; however, their attention was captivated by the other half of the species—girls . . .

Stooping back down to continue picking, Jim shook his head. *Girls.* They were a mystery that Jim didn't understand—nor had any particular interest in investigating. There were certainly other things to occupy his thoughts as adulthood seemed to loom on the horizon.

As he grew older, Jim had promised himself that he would focus on getting a good education and helping the family keep up the farm. That was simply going to be the life he pursued. In the meantime, his friends fell in love daily with different smiling, giggly beings with long hair and long eyelashes.

But Jim, ever "way too practical," as his older brother often teased him, operated under his own motto: First things first. Finish high school, finish college, get a good job—and then, and only then, would he worry about finding a girl. Besides, so many of the girls he met were a dime a dozen . . . Secretly, Jim had long ago promised himself that if he ever did fall in love, it would be different—*she* would be different. She would be the most wonderful girl in the world, an Angel sent from God Himself.

Jim went back to work, chuckling a bit. He wasn't sure if he believed in God or not, but, as far as girls and Angels went, Jim Palmer decided that he would just leave that one up to Him . . .

In terms of flavor, Jim knew he was vanilla. He would not have stood out in a crowd. He was neither unattractive nor superbly handsome. He wasn't challenged, nor was he a brilliant genius. Jim Palmer was not a social outcast, nor a homecoming king. He felt no need to express his manhood through drag-racing muscle cars, smoking behind the barn, or drinking with friends as did many men of his era.

He was ordinary, and it wasn't that there was anything wrong with being ordinary, Jim often reasoned. It was just that he secretly wished that he—just once—could be part of something extraordinary . . .

And Jim wasn't alone. Only miles away from his world, Pat Oswald found herself, too, wishing for something more . . .

Pat was surviving her teenage years, as do most girls that age, by consoling herself with the good things she had going for her. While boys continued to terrify her, Pat Oswald had close girlfriends, a cool older brother who, by then, could drive her to school. School was, for the most part, just okay. What to wear each morning continued to occupy a great deal of Pat's day-to-day thoughts, and, of course, the first day of school each year was a major event for her and her best friend, Debbie: *What would the cool girls be wearing? Would they finally be invited to sit at the prime lunchroom table?*

Looking back, Pat often chuckled in amusement at her preoccupation with her looks during those years. It was the era of sleeping on brush rollers with pointy, pink picks leaving dents in her scalp every night, dealing with routine teenage acne, and weighing a weight that she would later give anything to weigh—

even though she was absolutely convinced she resembled a circus-lady at the time.

But in so many ways, it was a golden time, not only for Pat, but for most people her age across America. Everyone listened to the Beatles and sang along to "Help!" and "I Want to Hold Your Hand." Friday evenings were all about attending school games and the mixer-dances that followed them. For Pat and her girl friends, school dances were an exciting place to be—who cared that she didn't speak to guys and had no clue how to dance?

High school was a busy and happy time, too. True to being a girly-girl, Pat loved home economics class, reveling in cooking and sewing, and finding the perfect elements for decorating a room. She was active in Future Homemakers of America and was thrilled to be inducted into the National Honor's Society in her sophomore year.

She and Debbie spent hours on the phone each evening—not without a great deal of objection from Romaine.

Dreamily, the girls would plan their futures, making all sorts of plans for "chasing boys," particularly the men of their dreams. They would discuss how many kids they would have and where they each wanted to live. Pat's "dream guy" even had a name—Jim. He would be an attorney, and the two of them would live happily ever after in a shuttered Cape Cod home with a white picket fence and tulips blooming in the front yard.

In moments of quiet, however, Pat found herself saddened a bit. It all seemed pretty unlikely since she still wasn't speaking to guys. True, by her junior year, her confidence level may have made it possible, but by then it was too awkward to say "hi" to the guys she had ignored for the past five years! While Pat felt as though she were sitting on the sidelines, both of her older cousins had been named Gratiot County Bean Queen and Dairy Princess respectively. She had watched them date, choose wonderful lace and tulle strapless gowns and had assumed she would do the same as a teenager.

My grandma once said, "Oh, Pat will be an old maid," and, to tell you the truth, I thought it might be true as I grew older. I remember dreamily watching my older cousins get ready for prom and thought, "These are supposed to be the best years of my life . . . " But they weren't . . .

I remember my mom asking me, "Isn't there anybody you could go to prom with?" I could only think of one boy, but he only existed in my imagination . . . It seemed impossible that love, true love, the kind you read about in epic novels and see in the movies, would ever find me . . .

Not far away, Jim Palmer was getting ready to graduate from high school. He would later confess just how much he always admired his younger brother Ted, who was much more outgoing than himself. Ted was involved in sports, had a girlfriend all through his high school years, and a group of friends to hang out with on the weekends. To Jim, Ted's life was more balanced than his own, and some small part of him always longed to be more "normal" as a teenager.

"Teddy? That you?"

Jim smiled from his chair in the living room, hearing that old kitchen screen door squeak a bit on its hinges as it opened, announcing the arrival of his energetic younger brother, just home from a Friday night football game.

"Hey, Jimmy-boy!" Ted grinned as he bounded into the living room, tousling his older brother's hair before flopping down onto the sofa.

"Did you have a good time?" Jim asked with a smile, feeling years older than his age as he watched his little brother's face light up.

"It was great!" Ted exclaimed with youthful enthusiasm, as she launched into a detailed account of the evening. There had been cheering crowds, food from the concession stands, and, of course, Ted's newfound interest, girls.

Jim himself, true to form, had spent the evening pouring over his school books, trying to gear up for a test. It was his senior year, and somehow getting good grades seemed more important than ever as his goal was in sight. He wanted to attend Central Michigan University the following fall.

Jim felt a keen sense of duty, being the first and only one in his family to attend college, so he again promised himself that he would focus on schoolwork, even sacrificing evenings like this one, studying rather than enjoying a night out.

Besides, he reminded himself turning back to his studying as Ted bounded up the stairs, *First things first . . .*

CHAPTER THREE
He Tends Tulips

Jim graduated from St. Louis High School in 1967 and began attending Central Michigan University that fall. The admissions process, registering for classes, choosing a major, finding an advisor—all of these things were new to Jim and to his family support system in St. Louis.

Jim wouldn't have called his college experience a typical one. CMU was only fifteen minutes from his parents' home, so Jim became one of the commuter students, studying on campus during the day and working on the farm evenings and weekends.

After serious contemplation, Jim decided to follow his love of drafting, majoring in industrial technology with an emphasis in mechanical and architectural drafting. Since he showed little interest in any of the typical campus activities, he was content to live at home and help with chores there, remaining ever close to his family and in keeping with his sense of duty. No one was more pleased than the ever-doting Ida Mae, who made no secret of the fact that she always wanted to keep her sons close by.

As an adult with boys of her own, Pat found herself understanding Jim's mother's wishes more so than ever before. Suddenly, as if that realization was a wrinkle in the fabric of time itself, Pat found herself snapped back to the present, as she once again remembered that she was no longer a dreamy-eyed freshman at CMU, but a mother herself with hopes and dreams for her sons, much like those of Ida Mae. Almost as if on cue, the ring of her cell phone broke the silence of her car as she continued on her way to her Middle School Seminar. Pat smiled as she recognized a familiar number on the caller ID, it was her son, Matt.

"Hi, Honey," her own voice sounded bright and grown-up, jarring in contrast to the childhood memories she had just been lost in. She suddenly was fully back in the present, reminded that her own children's childhoods were far behind them as well.

"Hi, Mom," she heard Matt's voice reply. "Are you still going to be in town tonight?"

"I'm on my way right now," Pat answered. "I have to be at the meeting this afternoon and conduct a seminar, but then I'm free as a bird! We're still on for dinner, right?"

"I'm sure planning on it!" Matt said. "Heidi's going to be stuck at the hospital tonight, so it'll just be me."

Pat smiled into the receiver, disappointed at the thought of missing her daughter-in-law, but equally delighted at an opportunity for one-on-one time with her second-oldest son.

Pat arrived at the school shortly afterward and found herself in full work-mode, delighting in every moment of her chosen field. She had to admit, though, that she still felt that rush of nerves and adrenaline when she got up to speak, always feeling like she was still a learner herself. The butterflies in her stomach were still unmistakable, reminding her of the shy, quiet girl she had once been, but she had learned a great deal about presenting over the last five years from her friend and colleague, Carolyn. What a hundred blessings from God she had been!

As the seminar began, she looked at the faces of the nearly 100 middle-grades teachers and administrators sitting in front of her, their faces reflecting their eagerness to improve outcomes for their students. She was tempted to drift back to the past again, remembering all too well what it was like to be a young teacher: desperate to make a difference, all the while battling the responsibilities and realities of dealing with ten to fourteen-year-olds on a day to day basis.

Pat smiled warmly at them and began to speak, energized and focused by the fact that this was an important contribution to middle school leaders.

When the seminar was over, Pat found herself reflecting on the session as she and the other facilitators packed up the materials. It had been a good day, all in all, with the teachers eager to learn new strategies for reaching young adolescents, along with basking in the time to share with other colleagues.

Pat smiled in satisfaction once again at the sense of pride and accomplishment she felt in her work. Her reasons were simple and her motives pure. She simply liked knowing that she was making a difference in the lives of at-risk kids and the men and women who taught them. It was one of her passions. And she knew she'd been lucky to have her family's full support in those early years, never feeling as though she had to choose between which part of her life she loved best. She loved her life at work and she loved her life at home—life was wonderful!

She traveled the short distance to her hotel on the outskirts of Flint where she and colleagues would be spending the night, before continuing to work with the teachers the following day. Glancing at her watch, she decided to indulge in a short nap. Oh, Pat loved her work, but it was draining being in front of educators the whole day. She needed to take care of herself, and a nap was just what she needed to be ready to enjoy her evening.

First things first, as Jim would always say . . .

An hour later, Pat dressed in jeans and a casual white cotton knit top, and pulled out her well-worn navy sandals. It was a beautiful evening for a walk to the nearby restaurant where she was meeting Matt.

Pat drew a deep breath of the warm spring air as she stepped out of the hotel. It smelled fresh, clean, and full of anticipation, as only spring breezes can. Purple and pink tulips were blossoming all around her.

Pat could hardly wait to spend the evening with Matt.

They were so lucky to find each other, she reflected on her son and his wife's relationship as she continued her short walk. *If I looked a hundred years, I couldn't imagine anyone more perfect for Matt than Heidi.*

Matt had been married to Heidi for three years now, and she was in her final weeks of residency in internal medicine at a nearby hospital. Pat often shook her head in wonder at the skill required of them to balance their busy lives and the upkeep of their marriage, but they were handling the juggling act with grace and lots of love.

Matt, was Pat's second son, soon to turn thirty, and a solid, hard-working, friendly man with integrity and ambition. While he looked more like her with his fine, dark hair and sparkling eyes, his personality was truly a replication of his Dad's.

Pat arrived at the parking lot just as Matt was getting out of his pick-up truck. His long, lean stature made getting out of the big truck much easier than it was for her or for Heidi. As usual, Matt was neatly dressed in a golf shirt and jeans. Pat beamed with pride. He was one of those rare people who could work outside on the lawn all day and emerge without a speck of dirt on him.

"Hey, Mom!" he smiled, easing her into a bear hug. "I'm really glad you could spare some time for me tonight."

Pat chuckled at his teasing.

"Well, don't get *too* used to it," she joked back. "I am, after all, *very* busy and important."

The two fell into easy conversation as they were seated in the restaurant.

Of course, conversation with Matt is always easy, just as it always had been with Jim, Pat found herself reflecting.

Matt had been, in every respect, an easy child. From his birth with a short labor, to sleeping through his first night home from the hospital, on through his teen years, Matt had never given his parents a day of worry. Pat sometimes wondered if they had taken Matt for granted: sometimes easy kids who always seem to do the right thing get overlooked. She sincerely hoped this wasn't the case. He was a treasure, and she hoped he knew this.

Matt was now a landscape designer. Spring was a busy time of the year for him. He worked some out of his home, but much of the time he drove a distance to the landscaping business where he worked in Midland. Landscaping was a natural occupation for Matt. He had always loved working outdoors, especially with farm equipment, much to his Grandpa's delight.

He certainly caught the farmer gene from his Grandpa! Pat thought with an affectionate smile.

During high school, Matt had been active in the FFA and had worked after school and weekends for a local florist. While in high school, he purchased Grandpa Palmer's old Oliver 66 tractor and had completely restored it on his own time. It was both functional—he often used to help him in landscaping—and an attention-grabbing antique with its fresh paint job and decals.

It is funny, Pat thought, watching her son's eyes sparkle as he talked. *It's funny that sometimes you can almost predict what a toddler will do as an adult.*

Matt was one of those toddlers. At the age of three, he was already following his Dad around the house, watching and asking questions about how everything worked. In fact, Grandpa Romaine had once commented, "If that kid doesn't know something, it won't be because he didn't ask!"

Matt was always someone to get things done—first things first—so much like his Dad. He had always been mature beyond his years and seemed to feel more comfortable with adults than with kids his age as he was growing up. Little Matt Palmer seemed to love nothing more than spending time with his grandparents and helping on the family farm.

Matt was also reliable. Pat recalled the countless times that the family had relied on Matt to fix an appliance, take care of a chore, or find a missing item. He was the "go to" guy whenever anything needed to be fixed. He was undoubtedly the most organized of her guys and always knew where his various tools—along with everything else he owned—were placed.

Now, Pat counted on him to design and install her own landscaping. The previous fall he had planted hundreds of tulip bulbs for her and they were in full bloom at her St. Louis home.

"So, tell me," Pat asked, leaning forward in interest. "How are things at work these days?"

"Pretty good," Matt replied. "With this nice weather, we're getting lots of calls for estimates on jobs. I met with six customers today to take measurements and begin working on their designs."

"That's a lot, isn't it?" Pat asked.

"It's keeping us busy, that's for sure!" Matt sighed. "I do think the installation crew could work a little faster so that we don't have to tell customers that we're already scheduling into July."

Pat smiled, suddenly reminded of a family joke. Matt, ever-organized and efficient, *always* thought things should be done sooner than they were. In fact, his brothers often joked that Matt Palmer probably thought God Himself could have created the world in *five* days—rather than six—if He had just gotten busy and stepped up the pace a little.

Pat had to admit that it was probably Matt's only flaw. He was sometimes critical of others, but only because he was so well organized and efficient himself.

"Well, Karen is really liking what you did in their yard," Pat grinned, pleased that her friend was so satisfied with Matt's work. "I saw the bridge you designed and built. It's really impressive and looks just perfect down by the river behind their house."

Matt didn't even attempt to hide a proud grin.

"Good! I'm really glad. How is Karen doing, by the way? Are you two still having lunch every week?

Pat nodded as she took a sip of her ice tea, silently breathing a prayer of gratitude as she did every time she thought of Karen.

"Every week for fifteen years," Pat said, her voice drifting a bit, almost as though she were thinking aloud, "She has been such a good friend to me—I don't know what I would do without her!"

"Oh, before I forget," Matt said, suddenly snapping his fingers. "Heidi says 'hi' and said to make sure to tell you that you and she and Andrea are all booked for your spa day before Kevin's wedding."

Pat beamed, pleased all over again that her daughter-in-law and daughter-in-law-to-be had included her.

"Great! I'm really looking forward to that. How is Heidi doing these days? She must be eager to finish her residency."

"Yes, she is." Matt replied with obvious pride in his voice. "Only three and one-half weeks to go. Mom, she has worked so hard. She really deserves a break. Those nights being on-call are long and, lately, the hospital has been really busy."

"I really admire her determination," Pat said. "She is finally getting to do exactly what she's wanted since she was four years old, right?"

"Yup," Matt answered, then changing the subject, noted; "Hey, are those new earrings, Mom?"

So like him, Pat thought affectionately. *He never misses anything*!

"Yes, they are!" she responded, delighted that he noticed. "I am really liking the chandelier-looking ones these days. Oh! Speaking of which, does Heidi have her jewelry and her dress for the wedding yet?"

Matt nodded as he took a sip of his iced tea.

"Yes, she does. It's really pretty, and you're going to love it.

It's bright pink. I think, in fact, it's just about the color of the nail polish you are wearing. What's that called?"

"Nail polish colors are always named around a theme," Pat replied with a chuckle. "Like this one is called 'It's All Greek to Me.' But you're right; hot pink is definitely my color!"

"And you are all set with your tux, I'm sure," Pat added with amusement, again remembering his knack for efficiency.

Matt nodded.

"I picked it up last weekend and it's hanging in my closet—all set to go."

"The wedding's coming up so soon, huh?" Pat commented. "Some days, I can hardly believe our little Kevin is getting married!"

Matt threw his head back and laughed.

"*Little* Kevin? It sounds like he is a toddler. He is almost twenty-four, right?"

Pat laughed somewhat sheepishly. It was true—sometimes, it was hard to admit that her boys weren't so little anymore. In her mind, she often still saw them as they were back in the days of playing with Legos and trucks in the basement playroom.

"You and Heidi will be celebrating your three-year anniversary soon, right?" Pat asked, as Matt nodded in confirmation.

"I really think you are so good for each other. I did a pretty good job of matching you up, didn't I?" She teased.

"That you did, Mom! No complaints here!" Matt said with a smile. "Heidi and I *are* good for one another. She makes sure I'm doing more than just working all the time."

"She really balances me," Matt added, suddenly becoming more reflective. "I need that—and I think that she worries less and is more optimistic with me around. Believe me, we are both enjoying this part of our married life: we have time to travel, time to be together and we like working on the house together. But, hopefully, we'll be able to start having a family soon."

"Well, of course, I am not *at all* anxious to have a grandchild," Pat said with mock indifference.

"Oh no, *of course* not!" Matt grinned. "That would be so unlike you!"

The evening passed too quickly. Appetizers and side-salads made way for mouth-watering entrees, and soon, mother and son were trying to decide on whether or not to share a dessert. After weighing their options, Pat finally sighed, deciding against chocolate cake with creamy fudge filling.

Weight! A constant battle for as long as I can remember.

She was trying to take off a few more pounds before the wedding. She was always waffling between being at an appropriate weight, so clothes would look better on her and just eating whatever she wanted. She did love food. Pat knew it would help if she liked to exercise even a little bit, but that involved sweat, and that certainly was not her thing!

"Well, I probably should head out," Matt said reluctantly, pushing back a bit from the table. "I want to try to work a little on one of the designs tonight before I go to bed."

"Yeah, I need to get going, too," Pat admitted with a sigh. "I need to do some reading tonight for tomorrow's meeting."

The two walked to the parking lot together. Pat hugged her son, and he whispered in her ear, "Psst, I'll love you forever and three more days." It was an affectionate phrase that the family had whispered to one another for more than a quarter of a century. She smiled, warmed by her son's love, and started her short walk back to the hotel. The air was still warm and sweet with the scent of tulips and spring lilac blossoms. Her thoughts drifted to Matt and Heidi, delightedly blissful in their marriage. Was it just her imagination or did the tulips on CMU's campus bloom particularly brightly the spring that those two laid eyes on each other?

She, herself, had played a role in Matt and Heidi meeting. It was 1997 when Pat had experienced, what she would later dub, a stroke of genius. At the time, Matt had just completed his horticulture degree and was spending long hours working on a variety of landscaping projects. Pat had discreetly discovered that Matt really wasn't meeting any young women in his world of plants and designs, and she was pretty sure that he wasn't opposed to the idea.

The problem was, she surmised that, he simply wasn't finding any opportunities to meet girls his age. Pat, in typical fashion, decided to nudge fate a bit. Putting her creative talents to work, she made a poster with Matt's photo on it, along with a list of his qualities: kindness, integrity, intelligence, maturity—a hard worker.

And the fact that he is good-looking is certainly self-evident from the picture, she had reasoned.

The next day, by chance, she had asked one of the students who worked in her office at CMU if she knew of anyone who might want to date Matt.

"You know, I think my friend, Heidi, just might be interested in meeting Matt," Haley, her student assistant, instantly piped up.

"That's great!" Pat had replied with a laugh. "Did you show her my poster?"

"I sure did," Haley chuckled, a scheming sparkle in her eye, "And Heidi said that Matt should give her a call!"

"Okay!" Pat declared with satisfaction. "This could be good, huh?"

Haley herself is such a gem that Heidi probably will be, too! Pat found herself reasoning.

Later that same week, Pat handed a phone number to Matt and, after a bit of eye-rolling in his mother's direction, Matt had called Heidi. Pat had been thrilled to hear Haley's triumphant report the next day: "They talked for almost two hours!"

Matt and Heidi were married five years later, with a beaming Haley as Heidi's matron of honor. Pat was absolutely thrilled with the success of her matchmaking endeavor: helping two people find true love was her passion in life!

Heidi had later confided to her that the moment she'd first seen Matt was electrifying. Pat had smiled at her daughter-in-law's revelation, relating to that feeling all too well. The same exhilarating feeling had happened to her so, so many years earlier on the same campus that was the scene for Matt and Heidi's love story.

Pat paused a moment in her walk, realizing that she had arrived back at the hotel, but was not yet quite willing to go inside out of the warm spring night.

Reminiscing about Matt and Heidi's first meeting was suddenly pulling her back into the past once more, back to a beautiful day on the campus of Central Michigan University when her world forever changed . . .

Chapter Four
Girl Meets Boy

Time moves forward. Life goes on. Children grow and blossom into adulthood. Spring turns to summer. Tulips bloom in a seemingly-unending cycle. Despite all of life's change and uncertainty, you somehow find security in coming to understand who you are, and one day, as if by magic, you find yourself thinking that you have it all figured out. That life couldn't possibly have any more surprises in store for you. You might even assume that the road ahead is straight and unbending, stretching out in front of you like a bleak desert highway . . .

But then, you'd be wrong . . .

The morning sun was shining on a gorgeous October day in 1969, and the campus of Central Michigan University was dressed in breathtaking fall colors.

Pat drew a deep breath, inhaling the pungent fragrance of the maple trees on Warriner Mall.

This was her usual route to various classes sprinkled across campus, but today! Today, the world was ablaze with reds, golds, and oranges vivid enough to rival any New England postcard. It made the somewhat ordinary walk to class make Pat feel as if she were in some magical land over the rainbow. The fall colors glittered with a vibrant hue in the morning sunlight, starkly contrasted against a brilliant blue sky. Autumn had certainly reached its heights that year.

So different from my freshman year! Pat found herself thinking, recalling rainy days nearly every day throughout September and October during her first months on campus. Days like today were a welcome change from those days of walking across campus to class in the rain.

Pat was now six weeks into her sophomore year and actually found the three-block walk from her room in an older home on Lansing Street somewhat enjoyable—with the exception of the brutal schedule she had lined up for herself: four classes back-to-back on Mondays, Wednesdays, and Fridays. She went immediately from math, to nutrition, to political science, to sociology.

Pat shook her head. Sometimes her ambition was exhausting. Tuesdays and Thursdays were a little easier with only two classes on those days. This left her with ten hours a week to work in the Home Economics Department. The extra money helped with some of her college expenses.

Pat spent a fair amount of her time in Wightman Hall, an older brick building covered with ivy on the north end of campus. All of her Family Living courses were in the building, as was her part-time job working for two professors in the department.

Pat caught her reflection in the glass doors as she headed into Wightman Hall and made a face, pausing only for a second to scrutinize her appearance.

Debbie was forever telling her not to worry about her looks, but she couldn't help but feel a bit self-conscious as she smoothed an imaginary wrinkle in her navy and burgundy plaid cotton jumper, complete with a navy blue turtleneck and blue tights. She was, however, secretly very proud of the fact that she had made the clothes herself. She also still loved to bake and sew, just as her mother had taught her, in spite of Debbie's teasing that such an attitude was definitely behind the times for a college co-ed in 1969.

Pat paused a moment before entering the building, reluctant to leave the warm sunshine behind her. It was the sort of day that usually leads one to daydream, and Pat found herself thinking, as she often did about her future, what she wanted her life to be like . . .

Life hadn't, up to this point, turned out to be anything like she'd planned. Oh sure, college was wonderful—new friends, new things to learn . . . but Pat still found herself dreaming old dreams, along with battling old fears. She would've never admitted it to anyone—except maybe Debbie or Suezell—but men were on her mind quite a bit lately, more so than the usual distraction that made Pat and her friends giggle and daydream.

As she had since her childhood days of playing bride, Pat still longed for true love. It was the thing she wanted most in the world, but lately, it had seemed to be a distant unreachable illusion that was destined to find everyone else in the world.

The road before Pat seemed to stretch out in front of her, lonely and devoid of the sweet surrender of falling in love. It was something Pat was attempting to convince herself was satisfactory, but those attempts didn't seem to be working.

Pat sighed and pulled the doors open to enter the building.

Just another ordinary day in the life of me . . .

The day went quickly, as it often did when Pat was working in the Home Economics Department. She enjoyed the mindless tasks—making copies for a couple of the professors, running errands, and performing other office duties—they helped the day go by more quickly. As always, Pat found herself pleasantly surprised to glance at the clock only to realize it was time to head home.

She quickly gathered her books and handbag, and headed towards the second-floor stairs. Her thoughts were far away, already planning out her evening of homework after dinner with Debbie. She was just approaching the floor lobby area when she spotted him.

It was him. Jim. Jim Palmer. Even now, I find myself smiling at the memory of that electric moment that seemed to be suspended in time, as if the whole of the universe and God Himself paused to watch the scene unfold. There Jim was, sitting in a study lounge area, reading a paper or munching on an apple or catching up on homework—I don't remember what he was doing exactly, but I remember the way the light caught his eyes and hair, and I remember the way my heart caught in my throat when he glanced up, grinned at me and said, "Hey! Aren't you Pat Oswald?"

Pat found herself returning his grin with surprising ease, "And you're Jim, right? Jim Palmer?"

He nodded and smiled again as Pat found herself detaching from the scene for a moment, wondering if God had suddenly given her some sort of magical ability to speak easily with men. Did miracles like that still happen in 1969 Mid-Michigan? Her thoughts were whirling around in her mind like a violent tornado.

God gave Moses the same kind of miracle in the Old Testament, didn't he? I wish I could remember for sure. I just can't believe this is happening! Wow, he is so handsome . . . Wow!

Pat shook herself back to the present, determined to sort through the emotions and questions later, but it seemed as if the rest of the conversation with Jim Palmer was a blur. He mentioned his involvement with the Future Farmers of America and that he knew her brothers from that. His eyes grew tender when he expressed his sorrow over her brother, Tom. Pat took special note of his concern. The wounds from the loss of her brother who died in an automobile accident the July after she had graduated from high school were still fresh. The family still grieved the loss daily, and she had relied on Debbie to help her through the tough times. Pat noted that Jim's concern seemed real and genuine.

Pat felt as though some long-lost piece of her being had suddenly made its way back. Jim was standing right in front of her, easily exchanging conversation with her about their majors in college, fellow St. Louis graduates attending CMU, their favorite part of college life. It was a surreal moment of clarity, as giddiness bubbled beneath the surface—what an amazing man!

He's so sensible, so cute, and yet seems like a real professional . . . so perfectly right! Pat's inner monologue continued, as she outwardly chatted easily with Jim. *He seems to like talking to me, and I can't believe I didn't freeze up while talking to him! This isn't like me to be so comfortable! Who is this guy?*

The hands on the clock suddenly made Jim aware that he needed to get to class. Pat felt the tiniest jolt of electricity sear her spine as he grinned at her, the flecks of gold in his eyes twinkling as he said, "It was very nice seeing you, Pat Oswald. Maybe we'll run into each other again some time."

With a final grin, he was hurrying down the hall, books under his arm. Pat watched him go, vaguely certain that nothing in her life would ever be quite the same again.

Hours later, I was curled up on my bed, finishing up the last of the day's homework. Of course, I could barely concentrate; something soft, warm, and golden kept creeping into the edges of my mind as I replayed our conversation over and over again. I found myself in a sort of blissful disbelief that such a man really and truly existed! Something I couldn't name was settling around me like warm autumn sunshine.

I pulled a worn leather-bound journal out from my nightstand drawer and penned the words that were already etched onto my heart: 'Someday, I'm going to marry Jim Palmer . . . '

CHAPTER FIVE
Planting

Deep down—somehow, some way—I knew that Jim Palmer was the man of my dreams, the man I was going to marry. No, it didn't make any logical sense in my day-to-day existence. Compared to the scope and breadth of the rest of the world, my destiny and dreams of finding true love in my little part of the world seemed somewhat small and insignificant . . . but I just knew it was already decided: Jim Palmer was the man for me.

I knew that God had something special in mind, of course. But His timing and mine were definitely not in-sync—a frequent source of frustration for me and a constant test of my faith. Looking back, I realize that my impatience didn't make waiting for Jim any easier.

"Pat, are you sure about this? I mean, are you really, really sure about this?"

Debbie's voice seemed to pull Pat away from her daydream to the outcome of the current task at hand. The two girls were walking very, very slowly past Wightman Hall. Two weeks before, it had been the scene for Pat's fairytale encounter with the man of her dreams. But today! Today, as in every other day for the past two weeks, Jim Palmer was nowhere to be found.

"I don't understand it," Pat said in frustration. "This is the time he should be getting here for class. Where is he?"

"I absolutely can't believe we're doing this," Debbie muttered to herself, instantly regretting her words as she noticed the crestfallen look on her friend's face.

"Oh, Pat, I'm sorry. You know I didn't mean that. It's just that you've been trying to bump into this guy again for weeks now, and I hate seeing you so disappointed every time."

Pat sighed.

"I guess I *am* being a little ridiculous, huh?"

"No, no," Debbie protested, putting a supportive arm around her friend's shoulder. "You're just being you—tenacious, persistent, grab-life-by-the-throat YOU!"

Pat smiled at Debbie's accurate description. While men had always remained a mystery to Pat, there were times when she felt she could honestly take the rest of the world by storm if she put her mind to it.

Still, she hadn't expected that bumping into Jim now and then to be this difficult.

They were, after all, both taking education courses and classes in their respective majors, mostly held in Wightman Hall. How difficult could it be to see Jim Palmer between classes?

God, please let me see him again—please?

Months later, a dull gray sky hung over the campus of Central Michigan University, matching Pat's mood as she hurried toward Wightman Hall. It was a frigid Monday afternoon in early December, and somber skies had just begun to spit out icy pellets. A frosty wind was starting to kick up, a sure sign of an impending storm.

Pat frowned miserably. It was the kind of day in which she wished she was home, curled up under her favorite quilt, sipping hot cocoa and delving into a good romance novel. And yet here she was, visiting Wightman Hall before her next class in desperate hopes of running into Jim. The awful weather was definitely prompting her to promise herself it would certainly be the last attempt to find him. It had, after all, been months! Even the most persistent people had to know when it was time to simply give up.

Entering the building, Pat shook snowflakes out of her hair and scarf and climbed the stairs toward the second floor. Her plan, as always was to pretend to be dropping by the Home Economics Department—very conveniently located near the drafting area where she'd seen him before—and just happen to run into Jim Palmer.

Pat smiled in amusement as she pulled herself away from the daydream. That fantasy was fine for yesterday and every day for the months since her last meeting with Jim, but today! Today was the last straw. Today, she would search the halls in vain for him for the last time. Today, she would give up the fantasy, go home, make some hot tea and cry in disappointment on Debbie's ever-ready shoulder.

And then, out of nowhere, there he was. It was Jim Palmer.

Pat's heart skipped a beat as she moved closer to him. He was seated in the make-shift drafting area that was actually a lobby area on the building's second floor near the Home Economics Department. Many areas on campus had been turned into make-shift classrooms. The number of students on campus was growing rapidly in the late sixties and classroom space was in short supply.

Jim was sitting in the back row of what appeared to be an open lab. Fellow students around him were working independently on their various projects, so it was easy enough for Pat to make sure he saw her as she approached.

Glancing up from his work, Jim noticed Pat approaching him, turned on his drafting stool toward her and smiled brightly.

"Well, hi, Pat Oswald!" he exclaimed with delight.

Pat attempted to hide the fact that she couldn't breathe for a moment.

"Hi, there!" Pat said, amazed at her own voice, calm, bright and confident. She glanced in the direction of the front of the room where Dr. Lutz appeared to be grading papers and suddenly became concerned that she was intruding on a class.

Jim read her hesitant glance and responded, "Oh, no, it's okay for you to be here now. This is just a work time for some of us to catch up on a few more mechanical drawings."

"Do you want to sit with me for a while?" he asked, pulling up another drafting stool near him before glancing anxiously back at her. "I mean, if you have time . . . "

"Are you sure it's okay?" she asked, pleased at his offer and taking special note of the fact that he seemed to genuinely want her to sit with him.

"Oh, it's fine! People sit here with guys all the time." A mischievous grin suddenly spread across his face. "I mean, it *is* pretty hard to keep all the girls away while I'm working."

Pat laughed aloud.

"That must be pretty tough," she teased, their laughter putting them both more at ease. "I mean, with all the girls following you around all of the time."

Jim grinned heartily.

"Well, it *is* hard, but *somebody* has to do it, right?"

The two chuckled again for a moment before Jim asked, "Can you believe the semester is almost over?"

"Yeah, I can't wait!" Pat replied. "I will be so glad when exams are over. I have six of them in two days! How about you? You're, what—half-way through your junior year?"

As if I don't already know that. Pat thought to herself with amusement.

"Yep, and with the exception of my chemistry class, it has been a good semester."

"Oh, who do you have for chemistry?" Pat asked. My roommate has had to take it three times! I am avoiding the subject all together!"

"I have Dr. Benson," Jim replied. "He certainly knows his chemistry—it's me I'm not so sure about!"

Jim laughed.

"In general, though," he continued, "I am now taking mostly drafting classes and while I spend a bunch of hours at the boards, I enjoy it."

"So, what are you working on right now?" Pat asked, turning on her stool to look at his drawing in front of them.

Pat, of course, knew that it was unlikely that she would understand the drawing, but, on the other hand, she desperately wanted to keep the conversation flowing, so she could learn absolutely everything she could about the man seated next to her.

"It's an engine part of an automobile—like one they might use at Ford or GM," he explained, apparently pleased that she was interested. "It's designed to increase efficiency."

He pointed out a few details on the design, studiously explaining them to her in intimate detail. Pat looked on, soaking in every word and enjoying how absorbed he was in something he clearly enjoyed.

Then, Jim stopped suddenly, almost is if he remembered who he was: shy, somewhat reserved and a little surprised at how easily he was carrying on a conversation with the young lady in front of him.

He broke into a sheepish grin.

"But anyway, that's probably a lot more than you wanted to know about drafting," he laughed. "So, what are your plans for Christmas break?"

My heart was racing, and I was loving talking to the wonderful man in front of me . . . Was this really happening? It was like something out of a fairytale, wasn't it? And, at that moment, how could I have known that Jim was thinking the exact same thing . . .

Pat Oswald looked so beautiful, perched on the drafting stool, and Jim Palmer couldn't stop staring at her eyes, her smile, her hair, the curve of her face. He felt a burst of pride as he caught wondering glances from his classmates.

Who's the girl with Jim Palmer?

"Oh, I absolutely love Christmas," Pat was smiling warmly at him. "So, it's always fun no matter what we do. But I'll probably spend some time with my niece. She is one and a half now and so, so cute! In fact, I just bought her a pink, frilly dress for the holidays. I can't wait to try it on her! She's our little Angel."

Pat, in fact, looked like an Angel, sitting there across from him, and he couldn't believe that she seemed to be hanging on his every word. Jim sincerely hoped he wasn't gawking, but he couldn't stop staring—she was simply breathtaking, but in a completely genuine way.

Her eyes . . . it's almost as if they punctuate every word, and she absolutely sparkles when she's talking about her little niece . . .

The tiniest shiver went up his spine as an image of Pat holding a baby emerged in his mind. Flash frames of an imagined future with her suddenly swam before his eyes. This was dangerous territory . . .

Jim had to admit that the memory of his last conversation with Pat had crept into his thoughts often the past couple of months. He even wondered if he'd bump into her again and daily found himself scanning Wightman's hallways for her face each time he was in the building. It wasn't typical behavior for him—he knew that—after all, he really should be focusing on his drafting. But he couldn't deny that Pat entered his thoughts now and then, occasionally even haunting his dreams.

"Sounds like you're enjoying being an aunt," Jim replied, doing his best to focus on her words. In reality, all he wanted in that moment was to take her into his arms.

Where in the world are these thoughts coming from?

She laughed lightly.

"Oh, I absolutely love it!"

"It has to be hard for your sister-in-law, being alone as a parent," he continued, his voice softening with genuine concern. The loss was such a terrible thing. "Do you still see her often?"

"Oh, yeah," Pat replied with a nod. "We're very close, and I think she really likes being around my parents, too."

"It's difficult—especially around the holidays," she continued, a touch of sadness shadowing her face making Jim's heart ache just a little. "But we all work to make it fun for Angela. Do you have nieces or nephews?"

Jim smiled as he always did when he thought of his brother's two kids. They adored their Uncle Jim, and Jim doted on them with all the devotion of a father.

Tousled hair, sticky hands and toddler-sized hugs *did* make a fellow think about his future—a wife, a home, children—but it almost seemed too much to ask for—at least for now. After all, first things first . . .

"Yes, my older brother, Richard is married and has two kids. Dale is four and Annette is two. They are both so cute and lots and lots of fun!"

Something sighed longingly deep inside of Jim as Pat touched his hand and grinned.

"I'll bet you're good with them."

Pat was so special—that much Jim had already realized—but it wasn't just the way that she looked. There was something about her; something that made a guy want to protect and honor her. Jim sensed that she was both fragile and strong. She was feminine, pretty, sincere, and she clearly loved her family.

Is it really possible that my dream girl is sitting here across from me?

The easy-flowing conversation continued on for several moments with Pat and Jim each finding out more about the other and each secretly relishing being able hold up their end of the conversation.

But, after a few moments, Pat reluctantly rose to leave; after all, she did have a class in another building. The two bid each other good-bye, each expressing the hope that they would run into one another again soon.

It was, to anyone else in the universe, just another moment in just another dreary December afternoon. But Pat knew differently.

Something magical is happening . . .

Pat donned her coat and gloves and headed outside into the cold. The snow was starting to fall faster now, and icy gusts of wind might've chilled her to the bone any other day—but today! Today, she was filled with a warm glow as she replayed every word of the conversation with Jim in her mind over and over again.

It was as if winter had suddenly melted away into warm and beautiful spring; the grass was green and tulips were blooming. The afternoon suddenly felt as magical as Christmas itself as I recalled how it had felt to sit with him, finding out more about his life. Yes, it was almost Christmas, and I had received the perfect gift!

My dreams are coming true! Thank you, God . . .

And yet Christmas and New Year's passed without a call from Jim. Pat began to wonder if waiting for Jim would ever have a happy ending.

CHAPTER SIX

Waiting for Blossoms

Someone wise once said that waiting is perhaps the most difficult discipline to master; and I certainly didn't find it easy—after all, the man of my dreams was real and living and breathing on the same college campus that I was! We weren't star-crossed lovers, separated by situation, family, money or tragedy. We were perfect for each other. It was simply God's timing that seemed to be keeping us apart . . .

In my heart, I knew exactly what I wanted in life and who I wanted to spend it with. All I needed to do was give "destiny" a little push . . .

Time passed, and spring slowly melted into summer. There were still no "Jim sightings," or even a phone call from him. But what Pat lacked in patience, she made up for in determination. It was time to set a plan in motion.

"Would you look at all that food?" Debbie said, clucking her tongue in amusement as they put the finishing touches on a mountain of tasty entrees. "You'd think that the Queen of England was coming for a visit!"

Pat laughed aloud.

That summer, Pat was sharing a house next to the Student Book Exchange with Debbie and four other college girls. The weather for the coming weekend promised to be warm and bright, and Pat had enlisted Debbie's help to plan the perfect ploy: a cookout with music and food and friends . . . and, of course, Jim. Fortunately for Pat, one of her roommates had graduated from high school in the same class as Jim and had agreed to make sure he was on the guest list.

Debbie and Pat had made elaborate plans for the party, using every one of their home economics skills, cleaning and decorating the modest rental house, along with preparing countless salads and carving artful watermelon baskets.

The food display *was* a pretty impressive spread, especially for college kids. There were appetizers, meatballs, assorted meats on the grill, salads of every kind and an appealing array of desserts and fruits.

Pat was desperately trying to ignore the butterflies in her stomach, hoping against hope Jim would show up tonight. After all, wasn't the whole point of this party to impress him?

As if reading her thoughts, Debbie remarked wryly, "I sure hope this Jim fellow is duly impressed, Pat."

"Me too," admitted Pat, growing a little starry-eyed as she continued. "But you know how I feel, Deb. I just have a feeling about him. He's *the one*. He's my dream guy."

Debbie's eyes softened in understanding.

"I know, I know," she said with a smile. "And everything is going to be perfect tonight, I promise!"

Pat knew that Debbie would follow her lead to the ends of the earth, including everything imaginable in planning and scheming ways to build a relationship with Jim. But Pat couldn't help but notice worry reflected in Debbie's eyes.

She's afraid I'll be disappointed . . . She's afraid I'll get hurt . . . But even if I do, it's worth it . . .

"Well, that does it," Debbie announced, changing the subject as she set the last appetizer on its tray. "Come on, Pat, let's go get all beautiful for our guests!"

The two climbed the stairs together, chatting and giggling.

Pat could barely contain her excitement of what the evening might hold.

The sky was a hazy blue, and the air was soft and cool for a July night, not too humid, not too hot. It was a gorgeous night for a party. Pat smiled in satisfaction as she surveyed the yard. It wasn't a beer bash or anything like that, just a fun group of college kid friends who didn't need drugs or alcohol to enhance their fun.

A couple of hours into the evening, and the party seemed to be a complete success. Guys and gals were spread throughout the house and backyard, talking, laughing and playing games.

"Pat Oswald, I presume," Pat heard a familiar voice behind her as she refilled a tray of appetizers. She flushed in delight, but quickly steadied herself before turning around.

"Jim!" she exclaimed. "What a pleasant surprise!"

"It seems we have a mutual friend," he said, nodding toward Pat's roommate. "What a coincidence, huh?"

Pat laughed in delight, silently promising herself to some day tell him about her elaborate plan to make sure he was there that night.

Jim Palmer is so handsome, she noted with what she hoped was an inaudible dreamy sigh. She took in his soft, yellow-buttoned oxford cloth shirt and khaki slacks, looking neat and pressed as always. And Pat loved his wavy, reddish hair and healthy suntan from work on the farm. His warm smile revealed two front teeth ever-so-slightly overlapping.

But mostly, she loved Jim Palmer's eyes. They were blue-green and alive with sparkle. He seemed to love talking to her, and it was becoming more and more obvious that he also enjoyed teasing her.

"So, this is quite a party—one of your home economics projects no doubt?" He teased her with a smile.

"Yeah," she retorted. "And, while I'm thinking of it, I'm going to need you to fill out an evaluation form on the way out. It could help my grade in the class!"

"I'll be sure to do that. And did you also make your outfit, Miss Becky Home-Ecky?"

"Actually, I did!" Pat replied, laughing as she glanced down at the blue and green culottes she was wearing.

"I'm impressed!" Jim responded, his eyes twinkling. "I'm afraid it's pretty difficult for me to get much practical use of my GM engine drawings yet."

"Ah, but you might decide to build your own car, right?" Pat added, tilting her head flirtatiously.

"I doubt that," Jim laughed. "But I actually *do* want to build my own house some day!"

"Really?" Pat asked, her eyes widening in admiration. "That's a pretty impressive goal!"

"Well, first I have to finish college," Jim explained with determination, suddenly turning more serious. "First things first. Then, I can pursue other things."

He smiled.

Pat could barely hear the drone of the party over the beating of her own heart . . .

Hours later, the party drew to a close, and Pat found herself in the kitchen alone, humming some nameless tune as she put leftover food into the refrigerator. What a perfect evening!

"Well?"

Pat turned at the sound of Debbie's voice behind her.

"Well, what?" Pat asked, a mischievous light in her eyes.

"Well, how did it go with Jim?" Debbie said in exasperation, pulling Pat toward a kitchen chair. "I saw you two talking all night, and I'm dying to hear the details!"

Pat laughed and began recounting the conversation. Even then, it all seemed to be straight out of some romance novel: the easy conversation, the warm summer night air, Jim looking handsome, and Pat giggling in delight over his every word . . .

"Well, this is it," Debbie said decidedly. "He has to call this time. He just *has* to!"

Pat smiled dreamily.

Of course he would . . .

The summer passed, and Pat was genuinely perplexed. It seemed that Jim had truly enjoyed talking to her. He had, after all, talked to her more than anyone else at the party, and he didn't appear to be dating anyone else. So, why didn't he call?

Frustrated and annoyed at what should have had a more predictable outcome, Pat decided once again to forget about true love and just concentrate on her classes.

If only it were that simple . . .

But then again, Pat was taking eighteen credit hours every semester, and it was even beginning to look like she could graduate a semester early if she took a couple of classes the following summer. The end was in sight.

It was December of 1970 when I next had a chance to talk with Jim. I remember my heart fluttering, a smile spreading across my face when I spotted his smile among the sea of faces in the crowded hallways. It was always totally unexpected when I saw him, a beautiful, wonderful surprise that brightened my day.

It was as though I were a child seeing a rainbow, taken by complete surprise with the wonder and beauty of it all, just as dazzled as the first time I laid eyes on it.

Wightman Hall was crowded, but Pat easily recognized Jim Palmer's copper-colored head as he sat in the lounge area, reading *CM-Life*, the campus' newspaper.

Her heart skipped a beat, and she once again found a childlike faith in miracles renewed.

Thank you, God! she whispered, drawing in a deep breath as she approached him.

"Hi Jim," Pat called with a smile. "It's been a while!"

Jim looked up, a bit startled. Then, a delighted smile spread across his face.

"Oh, hi, Pat!" he exclaimed, folding his newspaper closed to give her his full attention. "It's great to see you. It *has* been a long time. What have you been up to?"

Pat took a seat on the sofa near Jim.

Okay, don't sit too close, she told herself, squelching the nervous energy threatening to bubble over. *Just a "friends" kind of close . . . After all, he hasn't called . . .*

Maybe, after all, we could be just friends. It wasn't what I wanted—not at all, but he didn't seem to be interested. How could I have known he was thinking just the opposite?

Jim Palmer had scarcely stopped thinking about Pat Oswald since their last conversation the previous summer. He had been unable to believe his luck when he had arrived at the cookout and spotted her. He had enjoyed talking to her, teasing her, hearing her thoughts on the world. There was just something about Pat Oswald.

And yet the whole situation frustrated him to no end. Despite his resolve to focus solely on his studies, he'd been trying to run into her again for months. But it seemed that Pat did not appear on cue. In fact, he had just about resigned himself to the fact that she seemed to have vanished from CMU's campus altogether, but today! Today, the sun was sparkling on a fresh snowfall, and the world suddenly became brighter when she appeared out of nowhere.

"Oh, the usual, pretty much," she was replying lightly. "Just classes and homework and working in the department. How about you?"

"Pretty much the same," he nodded in understanding, suddenly wishing he wasn't so consumed with his studies. He was slowly beginning to understand his friends leaving homework unfinished in favor of the local drive-in, cozy in the front seat with Cokes and a cute girl.

Sometimes he even let his mind wander, imagining himself sitting at the drive-in with Pat. In his mind, she was always smiling at him as she snuggled closer under his arm, leaning her head against his chest.

This is dangerous thinking, he thought, fighting off a surge of panic at being lost in fantasy. He forced himself to focus back on their conversation.

"I have five classes right now and will be student teaching before long."

"Wow, that's great!" she replied with a smile that tugged at his heart. "I can hardly wait to be out there teaching for real."

"It will be different, that's for sure—and a little scary, too," Jim admitted. "But you! You with your impressive skills? You'll do just fine," he added, hoping that she would catch his reference to their summer conversation. Had it really been months ago? It seemed to replay itself over and over again in his mind daily.

"Thanks," Pat said, looking a little wistful before she caught herself. "I mean, I hope so!" She then smiled shyly and added, "I thought about you the other night as I watched the draft lottery on television."

I was desperately hoping I didn't sound like a stalker. How could I possibly explain to anyone how often Jim crept into my thoughts? How could I even explain it to myself?!

Pat felt herself flush a bit, realizing she may have revealed too much.

"What's that like for you?" she asked, ducking her head a bit shyly at her blush. "I mean, what's it like waiting to see your birthday come up on the screen?"

"Well, it's nerve-wracking, to be honest," Jim replied, worry marring his usually easy-going grin. "I was just sitting there waiting and feeling like my fate was in the hands of the game of chance. I've always been able to get a college deferment up until now, but this changes everything. I mean, if your number is a low one, you might as well pack your bags for Vietnam."

"Wow, I can only imagine how that must feel," Pat responded, a lump of fear suddenly tightening in her throat.

"The whole war seems so pointless and unending. What are we really doing over there anyway?" She added, feeling sad and frightened for them all.

"Actually, I was fairly lucky this time," Jim replied, seemingly reminding himself not to worry. "My number was 173—that doesn't guarantee that I won't be called up, but it does mean that it isn't a certainty like it is for those guys with numbers under 100."

"Oh, that's really, really good," Pat said, immediately hoping she hadn't sounded too relieved and overjoyed at the news.

"Yeah, I *am* lucky," Jim said, raising his eyebrows, seemingly intrigued by Pat's reaction and what it might mean.

Then he grinned at her, a simple easy-going, heart-melting grin that told her so much: that he liked that she had thought about him, and that she was clearly glad he didn't appear to be headed for boot camp for so, so many reasons.

As always, their conversation ended too soon, but Pat left Wightman Hall feeling a renewed hope for a relationship with the man of her dreams. She was also anxious to return to her room and check the newspaper. Using the draft system, the 173 would tell her his birthdate.

Fifteen minutes later, Pat rifled through the paper and found the listing: 173 meant his birthday was only weeks away—the day after Christmas, to be exact.

She smiled. It was perfect. He was a perfect gift from God at Christmas!

Christmas came and went, and I'd be lying if I didn't admit that my faith was wavering a bit. It wasn't supposed to be this difficult, was it? Perhaps a coming year of life without Jim was the reality I was destined to face. It was hard to think about. The fleeting glimmers of hope throughout the past year had apparently only been leading up to the ultimate heartbreak.

But then, as always, God had other plans in mind. The next time I saw Jim was in January . . .

"I can't believe we're doing this *again*," Debbie was chuckling wryly. "I mean, *seriously!* How many parties is it going to take to impress this guy?"

Pat had to laugh in agreement at her friend's observation, but this was an opportunity too good to miss! A late-winter twilight glimmered on the horizon, and the forecast was calling for mild temperatures and a light snow—all of the perfect ingredients for a winter party.

She and Debbie had planned for the party to be held at the Oswald farm, and she had enlisted the use of her brother's snowmobile. If all went right, Pat would have Jim's arms around her before the evening was done, even if it was only from the necessity of hanging on during an evening ride through the snow.

Not quite a romantic winter horse-drawn sleigh ride, Pat reasoned, *But hopefully, it will be just as effective.*

"So, we meet again," a familiar voice said with a chuckle. Pat felt her frozen cheeks grow warm as she turned around to see Jim Palmer standing there, bundled up in a dark wool coat and mittens against the frigid night air.

The party was in full swing and, once again appeared to be a success. A group of friends were building a lop-sided snowman nearby, while others were in the throes of a full-blown snowball fight.

"Well, hello again," Pat replied with a bright smile. It hadn't been that difficult to make sure that Jim was invited to this party, and now, as he stood there, grinning at her, she was so glad that she had.

"Funny that we bump into each other every couple of months," Jim was saying. Was that a twinkle in his eyes?

Pat laughed.

"Yeah, you'd think that on a small campus, we'd see each other everywhere," she agreed, before nodding her head in the direction of the snowmobile. "So, Jim, are you up for a dangerous, thrill ride? Everyone has to go on one before they can have one of my specialty blondie brownies."

Jim feigned a look of terror.

"Will *you* be driving? I'm not sure how safe this will be . . . "

Pat threw her head back and laughed as she and Jim got onto the snowmobile.

"Don't worry, Jim Palmer," she said reassuringly. "I haven't lost one yet!"

The night air was crisp, and the stars sparkled overhead in a canvas of midnight blue as Jim and I raced through the open fields surrounding my parents' home. A thrill shot through me as Jim's arms tightened around my waist, and we laughed with delight as the snowmobile sailed over bumps in our path, skimming with ease across the drifted waves of snow. I'll admit that at one point, I almost turned the machine over as I attempted to maneuver a sharp turn, but it didn't matter—I did, after all, want this ride to be memorable. As I felt the warmth of Jim's body against mine, I knew that it was definitely an evening to remember . . .

The hour grew later and the weather colder, and soon everyone was ready to head inside for hot chocolate and the warm pile of blondies. They were Pat's specialty and a source of pride, brimming full of chocolate and oozing butterscotch chips. They had never failed to win over even the pickiest connoisseur.

Jim was enjoying his second blondie as he said to Pat, "Those home economics skills of yours are coming in handy again. These are really great!"

"Thanks," Pat replied, smiling blissfully. Ah, the blondies—they never missed!

She was a little surprised at how connected to him she felt. It was as if they had their own inside joke—one that they shared privately, just like a real *couple*. And yet, as much as she wanted to put the world on hold and daydream on that particular thought, she knew she had to play hostess now. Daydreaming would be saved for later.

"Okay, everyone," she called out to the room full of slowly-thawing friends. "Want to play some games?"

Pat's suggestion was met with hearty agreement. The group spent the evening playing a variety of games, some of them silly ones, just for fun.

One game involved blindfolding a participant, good-natured Jim was selected for this one. He was twirled around a few times and then asked a variety of questions before being asked to take off something he hadn't worn to bed the night before.

Jim looked a little puzzled but responded by removing his shoes. When asked to take something else off that he hadn't worn to bed the night before, he removed his belt. This continued as everyone laughed, including Jim, who was clearly enjoying the fun. Jim ended up removing a number of pieces of clothing, including his shirt, before it occurred to him to remove *the blindfold*!

As he realized the punchline, he laughed sheepish, taking off the blindfold. Everyone applauded as he took a good-sported bow.

It was funny, but I was more certain than ever that Jim Palmer was the man I wanted to spend the rest of my life with. He was truly a dream come true! And it seemed odd to me that he didn't seem to have any idea how handsome he was, or even how much I appreciated and admired his maturity, for that matter. He was different from other men that I had known. He was modest, lacking an ego the size of Cleveland, unlike most of the men I had met on campus.

He wasn't particularly into sports, nor was he an intellectual snob. Jim possessed practical knowledge of just about everything, but more importantly he was wise. He was solid, sincere, sweet, and genuine. He was exactly the kind of man every girl secretly wishes to marry. Someone capable of great and lasting love.

Now, if only I could find a way to get him to ask me out. If he showed even the slightest spark of interest, I would have waited forever. But forever seemed like such a long time to wait . . .

Not far away, Jim was driving home from the party, replaying the evening in his mind, along with the conversation he had shared with Pat. There was no denying the special connection between the two of them, and he desperately wanted to be with her, talk to her, touch her, hold her and kiss her for hours at the drive-in. All of the things his friends obsessed over suddenly made perfect sense. The light in Pat's eyes and the curve of her face nearly drove him to distraction when she was around, and threatened to break his ironclad 'always be a gentleman' policy.

Pat Oswald was just special, so feminine, soft and sweet; and he loved the way she made him laugh, and brought vibrancy and energy to his sensible, somewhat structured existence. A woman like Pat was exactly what he'd been searching for his entire life, and the internal struggle each time he laid eyes on her was almost more than he could bear.

He sighed as he turned into the driveway of his parents' home. A perfect evening was over, and he simply couldn't get involved with a woman right now—*any* woman—no matter how special or perfect she was.

So, Jim Palmer resolved once again to focus on finishing his degree, his pragmatic side prevailing as always.

After all, he reminded himself. *First things first.*

But somehow, this time, his mantra rang hollow, and a world without Pat Oswald seemed empty and meaningless.

Jim sighed again.

But first things first . . .

The weeks passed slowly. Pat kept waiting for Jim to call. Jim continued to attempt to focus on his studies in between daydreams of a life with Pat. Two young people were spending their days and weeks working and studying not too far away from each other, both continuing to thrill over the prospect of occasionally seeing the other.

Pat chaffed at the frustrating nature of it; after all, this wasn't some Shakespearean play. Just *how difficult* was it going to be to date Jim Palmer?! *That* she didn't know, but Pat Oswald was determined to find out once and for all.

Pat had learned during the winter party that Jim was doing his student teaching at St. Louis High School, alma mater for both of them. This information was invaluable. Now, she could engage Suezell to help her with her next scheme.

"Suezell, please?" Pat pleaded. "This is really, really important!"

"But, Pat—" Suezell protested.

"All you have to do is tell him that I said 'hi' when you see him at school," Pat interrupted, urgency creeping into her voice.

"But Pat, I'm just a *high school junior*, I can't just go talk to a *teacher*!"

"But you're also an office aide," Pat insisted. "Just tell him I said hello when you go get the attendance slips from all of the classrooms."

Suezell looked doubtful, her painfully shy side making the

whole scheme sound like a torturous plot.

Pat's tone suddenly softened.

"Please, Sissy?" she asked, her pleading eyes threatening to spill over with tears. "I'm at the end of my rope with this guy, and I'm so crazy about him! I don't know what else to do!"

Suezell put an arm around her sister's shoulder, her resolve growing.

"Okay," she announced firmly. "I'll do it. After all, you'd do this for me, right?"

Pat pulled her little sister into a hug.

"I would! I promise! And thank you!"

A week later, Pat was sprawled across her bed studying when the bedroom door flew open.

"Well, I did it!" Suezell stated proudly as she strode into the room. "I told Jim you said 'hi!'"

Pat's face broke into a grin.

"What did he say?" she demanded expectantly.

Suezell flopped down on the bed next to her sister.

"Well, he got this big smile on his face and said something like, 'Oh! Well, thank you for passing that along, Miss Oswald. Tell her I said hello right back.'"

Pat squealed in delight.

"Perfect!" she exclaimed. "Okay, now on to phase two of my plan . . ."

"Wait a minute," Suezell protested. "I thought all I had to do was say hello."

"You're right," Pat agreed with a nod. "But I think I should start picking you up from Pom practice."

Suezell broke into a chuckle, suddenly understanding where her sister was going with the thought.

"After all," Pat added, a mischievous glint in her eyes. "What are sisters for?"

The late spring breeze was warm and gentle, carrying the

scent of wet earth and new blossoms in its wake. Tulip gardens were full of color, and the afternoon held all the promise of new love about to bloom. It was early May in 1971, and Pat found herself sitting in her parked car, anxiously tapping her fingernails on the steering wheel.

Following her latest plan, Pat had finished her last CMU classes of the day and had driven to St. Louis High School. A little amazed at her own bravery, she had pulled into the parking lot just before school let out, found Jim's car and eased her car into the space next to it. Time ticked by slowly, and she found herself dozing off into a dreamy sleep.

Pat awoke with a start to the sound of a horn blaring from the nearby road. Groggily checking her watch, she realized she'd been sitting in her car waiting for nearly two hours.

Later, she would find out that Jim had been dedicatedly working on lessons and grading papers before he left for the day. Fortunately, Pat's stubbornness and persistence made her resolve to stay put until Jim emerged from the school.

Moments later, she spotted Jim Palmer striding across the parking lot at last, seemingly lost in thought. He was nearly to his car when he noticed Pat.

"Pat!" he exclaimed in surprise, a delighted smile spreading across his face. "What brings you back to St. Louis High School?"

"Oh, I am waiting for my sister to get out of Pom practice," Pat replied, silently praying for forgiveness for her tiny white lie.

"Oh yeah—Suezell, right?" he replied with a grin. "I see her when she picks up attendance slips every day. She says 'hi' for you."

"So, how's your semester going?" he added. "It's almost done, right?"

"Yes, thank goodness!" Pat sighed. "How about you? You graduate in a couple of weeks, right?"

He nodded.

"Yeah, it looks like I'm going to make it—amazing, huh?" Jim said laughing. "Four years do go by quickly. It's a little surreal to finally accomplish something that I've worked for for so long."

"I know what you mean," Pat said with a nod. "I can hardly believe that I'll be student teaching in the fall, and then it's graduation time!"

"You're finishing a semester early?" Jim said, his eyebrows raised in surprise. "That's great!"

"Yep," Pat confirmed. "If I take two Phys-Ed classes and one Sociology class this summer, I can graduate early."

Pat was desperately trying to focus on their conversation but found herself lost in his warm eyes.

We'll be graduating the same calendar year, she thought with an internal dreamy sigh. *The perfect time for a life together to begin. I wonder if he's noticed that I'm wearing contact lens. I wonder if he likes the way I look without glasses.*

"Hey, did you get contacts?" Jim's voice interrupted her thoughts, as if on cue. "You have always worn glasses, haven't you?"

"Yes, I finally got rid of those awful things." Pat said, ducking her head shyly.

"Well, I thought your glasses were just fine," Jim protested. "But the contacts *do* accent your eyes more, *I* think."

"So, then that's a good thing?" She asked, smiling warmly at him.

"That's a very good thing." Jim grinned.

Chapter Seven
Someone

'A very good thing' . . . Those words from Jim Palmer would've been enough to keep me blissfully in love for a few months more of waiting for Jim. But it seemed that God's plan had at last aligned with the magical destiny that I knew was meant to be all along. At last, my dreams were coming true . . .

"Something wrong, Pat?"

Pat glanced up from the dishes she was washing to see Suezell standing in the doorway watching her.

"I'm fine," Pat sighed, feeling as though the farmhouse kitchen was a prison.

"You don't *seem* fine," Suezell commented, picking up a dry cloth and setting to work on a pile of steaming plates.

"So what?" Pat snapped.

"Hey!" Suezell retorted defensively, irritation in her voice. "Why so grouchy?"

"It's just that this summer is going to be so depressing," Pat said with a disheartened groan. "Oh, sure, Deb and I will do things together, but now that you have a guy, I'm stuck being the older sister with *zero* going on in my life!"

Suezell was silent for a moment before patting her sister's shoulder sympathetically.

"Maybe your summer will surprise you," she said softly, breathing a prayer that it would be true.

Pat turned back glumly to the task at hand.

Of course, life has a way of surprising you. It's the thing that beautiful songs, great operas, romance novels and fairytales are made of. But would it ever happen to me? I was beginning to doubt it. Then, the phone rang. In that moment, everything in my world changed.

"Hello?" Pat said politely into the receiver.
"Yes, could I speak with Pat Oswald please?" a familiar voice said.
"This is Pat," she replied, still uncertain as to who was on the other end of the line.
"Pat, this is Jim Palmer."
For a moment, Pat couldn't speak or breathe.
JIM IS CALLING ME!!!
"Uh . . . Hi, Jim," she finally managed, fighting to regain composure. Was this a dream? Could he really be calling at last?
"So, how are you?" he asked in a friendly tone.
"I'm fine," Pat responded, at last able to breathe normally. "Just washing some dishes . . ."
Did I really just say that? Please tell me I didn't really just say that . . .
Pat heard Jim laugh.
"Ah, those home economics skills are coming in handy again." he said with a chuckle.
Pat felt relief spread through her as she instantly relaxed.
"Well, I have to keep my skills sharp, you know," she teased with a laugh. "What are you up to?"
"Well, I graduated last week!" Jim said. "So, I've really just been job hunting."
"That's great!" Pat said brightly. "Congratulations!"
"Thanks," Jim responded, a smile in his voice. "It's nice to have one more thing crossed off my life to-do list."
Pat laughed again.
"I can hardly wait to do that myself!"

"Anyway," Jim said, clearing his throat. "I wondered if you'd like to go to the show tomorrow night?"

JIM PALMER JUST ASKED ME OUT! I must be dreaming . . . Can this be really happening? What am I going to wear? What will we talk about? I can just see us now, cuddled together in the car. He'll put his arms around me, look into my eyes, and kiss me until I can't breathe.

"Pat?" Jim's voice suddenly sounded nervous. "Are you still there?"
I haven't given him an answer yet—say something, Pat!
"Sure," Pat heard herself say, surprisingly calm. "That sounds great!"
"Great!" Jim said enthusiastically. "See you then."

I hung up the phone and stood for a moment, frozen and speechless and so happy I wondered if I would burst from the excitement. A moment later, I noticed that my mother was standing in front of me, staring at me with concern.

Emerging from her trance, Pat threw her arms around her mother and laughed out loud.
"Mom!" she exclaimed jubilantly. "He finally called! He finally called!"
Naomi stared at Pat, speechless and uncertain what she was talking about. Suddenly Suezell appeared, drawn into the room by the commotion.
"What in the world—?" she said in confusion.
Pat grabbed her sister's arms and twirled her around the room until Suezell was laughing and breathless.
"Pat, what—?"
"JIM PALMER JUST ASKED ME OUT!"
Suezell shrieked in delight and clapped her hands.

"Really? He did? When?"

"Tomorrow night!" Pat exclaimed exuberantly. "Oh, this is the best day of my entire life!"

"Boy, that phone call sure changed your mood!" Suezell teased, flushed with the excitement of the moment.

Suddenly, the back door flew open and Pat's dad, Romaine, rushed into the kitchen.

"What's wrong?" he asked in alarm. "I heard screaming!"

"Nothing is wrong," Pat beamed. "The world is perfect! Jim Palmer just asked me out!"

Romaine let out a sigh of relief and chuckled in amusement.

"Well, I'd say that's good news then," he said with a pleased nod.

I am about to have the life I've always dreamed of . . .

"I have to call Deb!" Pat said suddenly, frantically dialing as her family went back to their chores.

"Deb!" she blurted into the receiver a moment later. "I'm coming right over to see you. I have the *best* news!"

The next day dawned warm and bright. A golden sun was shining, tulips and lilacs were in full bloom, and Pat Oswald was alive with nervous, excited energy. She woke up early, cleaning the house from top to bottom. Every pillow was fluffed and positioned perfectly, fresh flowers were arranged in a vase on the table, the area rugs were vacuumed, and the hardwood floor in the farm house living room was gleaming.

Later in the morning, Pat joined her parents and grandpa to attend the Highland Festival Parade in Alma where Suezell was marching and performing a pom routine. The sidewalks were lined with people enjoying perfect 70 degree weather. But Pat was barely conscious of her surroundings.

I have a date with Jim Palmer! He finally called!

But as evening approached, Pat began to realize that she had a problem. Yes, Jim had asked her to go to the movies with him, but, unfortunately, he hadn't indicated whether it would be the early or late show. Now, Jim could have asked her to a mud-wrestling tournament, and she would have been wildly enthusiastic about it, but the Strand Theatre in Alma had a seven p.m. and nine p.m. show, and now Pat was unsure exactly what time Jim Palmer would be arriving at her door.

Deciding to play it safe and be ready by six o'clock, Pat selected a new outfit to wear for the occasion: a blue-green short-sleeved knit top and a matching short skirt with brown circular patterns. She picked out light brown chunk-heeled shoes and sprayed on her favorite Avon cologne, *Occur*, before she surveyed herself one last time in the mirror. Her fine, brown hair was cut short and teased into a look that framed her face, lightly dusted with makeup.

As she scrutinized her appearance, there seemed to be a thousand things she would have changed in an instant, but suddenly a thought occurred to her.

Jim Palmer likes me! Just the way I am.

The reflection in the mirror suddenly seemed a little brighter.

Pat was dressed and ready to go by 6:30 p.m. Suezell pleaded to be allowed to be a part of things so Pat agreed to let her hide out of sight behind the living room's bookcases. Their parents had gone to see some friends and left well before Jim would arrive. Pat sighed with relief as the door closed behind them.

Time passed slowly, and Pat reasoned that Jim must have intended for them to go to the late show in Alma. Still, she sat frozen with anticipation in the living room chair for two more hours. Pat found herself growing a little panicked.

Did I only imagine that he had called? Was it just another dream about Jim?

At long last, Jim finally arrived about nine p.m. looking like a movie star and nearly taking Pat's breath away.

He smiled at Pat.

"Have you been waiting long?" he asked.

"Oh, no," Pat replied, once again breathing a prayer asking forgiveness for her white lie. "Just a few minutes."

I've been waiting for this moment for two years, actually, I've been waiting my whole life.

"Well, I thought we'd go to the Skytop Drive-In in St. Louis tonight," Jim continued as they walked out to his car. "And it was getting later and later, and it still wasn't getting dark yet! I guess that's Michigan in May for you, huh?"

That explains it! I can't believe I didn't think of that.

Climbing into his car, Pat followed through with a plan she and Debbie had devised and slid over to sit next to Jim. The pair made the short drive to the drive-in, parked the car, and arranged the speaker in his side window. For all Pat knew, they could have been showing college football. In fact, the film "Airport" flickered on the screen, but it didn't matter—Jim and Pat were completely engaged in talking about everything: graduation, job hunting for teaching positions in drafting, her plans to graduate in December once she finished student teaching, farming, kids they knew in high school and college.

The dam had been broken: two shy kids had blossomed into adulthood and were loving every moment of a truly magical evening. I remember being amazed at how comfortable it was. I felt I could tell him anything, and he would instinctively understand. I was overwhelmed by the growing attraction I felt for him. It was as if a powerful magnetic force was drawing us together.

After the movie, Jim suggested they visit a favorite hangout, the Alma A&W Drive-In. As they drank mugs of root beer, Pat secretly hoped old high school classmates would see her in her crowning moment of bliss. Everything during the evening had been perfect, except for one minor detail.

Nothing, absolutely nothing, could've torn Pat away from Jim's side that evening, not even the growing discomfort of a bladder nearly ready to burst. She had sat for two hours at home waiting for Jim's arrival, held it all through the movie, and now, a frosty mug of root beer later, Pat realized that she really needed to find a restroom in a hurry.

But if I walk away now, even for just a second, I could break the magic spell, and the fairytale might end!

So, Pat remained silent, hanging on Jim's every word and praying for bladder control.

The stars were shining brilliantly overhead as Jim drove Pat home and walked her to the door.

"Pat," Jim said, a smile lighting his face. "I had a really nice time tonight."

Pat beamed.

"I did, too!"

"Would you like to go out again next Saturday night?"

"I'd love to!" Pat smiled brightly, trying desperately to remain cool and calm.

His eyes met hers, and they stared at one another for a moment, smiling and resisting the desire building between them.

Then, his eyes twinkled.

"Goodnight, Pat," he said with a grin.

"Goodnight, Jim!" she replied softly.

Jim walked to his car, and Pat paused a moment to watch him drive away before flying into her house toward the bathroom, grateful it was located near the door.

As she emerged, she noticed her mother standing in the

hallway, pulling her bathrobe around her.

"Well," Naomi asked, a sparkle in her eyes. "Was it as wonderful as you thought it would be?"

"Even better," Pat said dreamily, giving her mother a peck on the cheek.

Naomi smiled warmly at her daughter.

"Well then," she said lightly. "I will see you in the morning—sweet dreams!"

Pat floated upstairs to the bedroom she shared with Suezell. She cracked the door open and slipped into the darkness quietly.

"Well?" a voice in the room demanded. "How'd it go?"

Suezell turned on the lamp and sat up in bed, staring at her sister expectantly.

Pat smiled, laughed and began twirling around the room.

"Oh, Sissy," she sighed happily to her younger sister. "We're going out again next Saturday!"

Suezell clapped her hands excitedly.

"I guess that means it went very well, huh?" she grinned.

Pat flopped down on her bed, staring at the ceiling dreamily.

"It couldn't have gone any better," she told her sister.

"So what was with the 'no, I haven't been waiting long' thing?" Suezell teased with a giggle.

Pat laughed out loud.

"By the way," Suezell added with a smirk. "I hope you know that I'm taking credit for all of this! After all, *I'm* the one who kept telling him you said 'hi' . . . "

"Fair enough," Pat beamed.

The two girls talked and giggled a few moments more as Pat shared every detail of the evening. Finally Suezell snapped off the light, and Pat drifted to sleep, blissfully happy.

My life has officially begun. I am who I was intended to be! God is so, so good.

Chapter Eight
Splendor on a Summer Day

The summer, as always, was going by too quickly, Pat mused, pulling herself back to the present once more as she took another sip from her morning tea. Birds were chirping brightly, the day promised to be warm and inviting, and Pat smiled at the way the sunlight was touching the trees outside.

Ah, today! Today was going to be a beautiful day!

And only two more weeks until the wedding, Pat marveled, making a mental note to call Kevin later on to check on his progress with the groomsmen gifts.

Pat knew there were other things she should be doing, but she had found it difficult to resist lounging with her tea a bit longer this morning. One of the benefits of being in education had always been some slower time in the summers. Although now, Pat was kept pretty busy in the Center during June, July, and August as well. Still, there was a lot more flexibility, and today was going to be a fun break from day-to-day work routines.

Today was Randy's birthday, and she was traveling to southeast Michigan to spend the day with him. It still amazed her that she, Pat, was driving to the Detroit area and didn't feel too panicked about it—certainly a change from days in the past when a trip to the Lansing Mall was a major ordeal.

Humans are amazingly adaptive, she thought, reflecting as she watched the hummingbirds hover over the tulips outside the kitchen window. *We all grow and learn to do new things throughout all of life . . . A constant transformation . . .*

Being able to drive without paralyzing fear was a new freedom for her, and she felt a sense of pride.

Her thoughts then turned to Randy's birth, as do all mothers on their children's birthdates. Randy had been born on the second day of their church's Vacation Bible School. Pat smiled with amusement, remembering that she had actually planned to co-direct the activities that year. Randy had certainly changed all of that.

She and Jim had been quite certain that Randy would be their girl. They had carefully paid attention to all of the timing issues and felt sure that Jeff and Matt would have a sister nine months later.

But what a wonderful surprise Randy had been. Pat thought with an affectionate smile. He was just as they had prayed for, exactly what God intended for them.

Unlike his two older brothers, Randy was born with lots of reddish hair. He was a beautiful baby and toddler. Strangers and friends alike would spot him and always remark, "Why, he's too pretty to be a boy!"—whatever that meant! Pat only knew that his wavy red hair, pudgy cheeks, freckles, and big blue eyes were adorable, and that she had loved him from the first moment she saw him.

Randy was unique from his older brothers in other ways as well. In fact, Jim and Pat often joked that God apparently didn't give couples two children alike because they might *actually* figure out how to parent them—*and what would be the challenge in that?!*

Randy had loved sports as a child and teenager, though Jeff and Matt had shown little interest. Randy played baseball and was a pretty good first baseman, a source of delight—not to mention a bit of a shock—to his athletically-challenged parents!

He absolutely loved basketball and had spent hours shooting hoops in the back yard. He went off to basketball camp in the summer, and was one of the few who then came home and religiously practiced shooting free-throws and other shots hundreds, and thousands of times every single day.

Pat smiled at the memory. She had loved watching Randy shoot three-pointers in high school—his form was perfect.

And while Pat couldn't actively participate in Randy's love of sports, she did love his interest in fashion. From the time Randy had been five years old, he had specific tastes (and very good taste at that!) in clothes and in how he looked.

He had starting using gel to style his hair in fourth grade, and he had been something of a trendsetter in their small Mid-Michigan community, folding his shirt collar up in the way that became so popular in the '80's and the early '90's.

Randy loved shoes, even more than clothes. Pat recalled, with a smile, that his favorite gift of all time had been a pair of very inexpensive red and black hightops that she and Jim had bought him for Christmas when he was in kindergarten. Jeff had recently helped Randy move and mentioned later to Pat that Randy must have transported more than a hundred pairs of shoes into his new home in Hazel Park.

Appropriately, today Randy and Pat would be meeting at an outlet mall near Pontiac. Both of them loved to shop and thoroughly loved finding bargains.

Randy had graduated from CMU two years ago with a business major and was working in insurance sales. This work, not unlike Jeff's, did not guarantee an income since it was completely commission-based. Sales, as most work in Michigan, had been challenging with the collapse of the auto industry. Pat was glad that today she would be able to purchase some clothes for Randy and take him to lunch. It would be good to spend time with him, and it was also a good way to support him.

Pat was turning into the massive parking lot when her cell phone rang. It was Randy.

"Hi Mom, where are you? I'm in parking lot E-5."

"Okay," Pat replied with a smile, veering her car into the

west entrance. "I'm just pulling in, so I'll come to that area and meet you in a minute—Happy Birthday!"

"Thanks, Mom," Randy said. "See you in a minute."

Moments later, they found each other and were headed to the entrance of the mall. It reminded Pat of the many trips that she had made with Randy, and, usually, his cousin, Eric, or another friend, to the shopping mall.

Pat suppressed a grin, remembering with a smile, the time when, as middle-schoolers, Randy and a friend had returned to the car after one such mall trip, wreaking of cologne. With careful questions, Pat had finally gathered that the two friends had tried a combination of every tester bottle in the department store! It had certainly been a fragrant ride home. In moments of quiet, Pat had to admit that she missed those days with her sons.

Moments like that pass much too quickly—as does life, she lamented silently.

Directing her attention to more pleasant thoughts, Pat glanced at her son as he held the Mall Entrance door for her. He was fashionably-dressed in a light blue checked Ralph Lauren shirt, a great color for his complexion and hair. He wore jeans and looked comfortable and stylish in one of his many pairs of shoes. A pair of his Michael Jordan remakes perhaps? At any rate, the light blue trim on the shoes actually matched his shirt. He was also wearing one of his gold bracelets.

This is my son, Pat thought, beaming with a renewed sense of pride. *He loves clothes as much as I do.*

"So, where do you want to start?" Pat asked him.

"I was really hoping to get some new jeans and maybe a couple of shirts," Randy said with all of the confidence of an experienced shopper. "So, Old Navy, T.J.Maxx, and Marshalls might be good places to start; but then there are lots of men's stores here to choose from."

"No, that sounds good, Randy," Pat replied. In truth, she

didn't care where they shopped; she was just enjoying the time with her son. "T.J.Maxx is right here, shall we start there?"

"Okay," was his simple reply.

Pat, as always, noted the difference between Randy and her other sons. He was definitely much quieter, although he was more talkative when it was just the two of them together. Perhaps, she reasoned, he found it difficult to compete with the other three brothers who were *real* talkers.

She glanced at him again as he carefully checked the price on several pairs of jeans. He was tall—a little over 6'1," and *too* thin, Pat thought, wishing she shared that trait with him.

"I guess I'll try on these two pairs," Randy finally said as he headed for the dressing room.

Pat nodded. "Okay, I'll just check on some of the home décor items while you're doing that. I know you have been looking for some black bath accessories for the new house. I will check to see what they have."

He smiled at her.

"Okay, I'll join you in a minute," he said holding up the jeans with a grin. "First things first."

A while later, they left the store with a pair of jeans and some black shower curtain rings Randy had been looking for.

"That's pretty cool that you found the black rings, Mom," he commented. "I think they'll look really good in my bathroom. You know, I painted the cabinet white and hung a black mirror above the vanity."

"How's the rest of the house coming?" Pat asked, as they made the short walk to the next store.

"Pretty good," Randy replied with a satisfied nod. "*And* it really was a great deal since it had been foreclosed."

"Absolutely," agreed Pat with a smile. "I think it was a great deal for a little bungalow; of course, it stills needs some serious cleaning and paint."

Pat paused a moment before adding what she hoped was nonchalantly, "I imagine Theresa will be anxious to see it again."

When Randy didn't respond, she prodded a bit more.

"When will she come home again?"

Randy smiled in amusement, refusing to take the bait.

"She's done teaching for the year, but she's staying in Arizona to do some curriculum work until the first week of July."

"Well, she really seems like a sweet girl," Pat said, trying once more to nudge the conversation to a more informative exchange.

"Yes, she is," Randy grinned, but the sparkle in his eye seemed to suggest that 'sweet' was exactly the right term to describe her.

"Okay, okay, Mom. Here's the deal," he finally relented, quietly chuckling in amusement at Pat's obvious curiosity about the situation. "We talk every night, but please don't go getting ready for another wedding just yet. You know she is teaching in Phoenix, and she does want to come back to Michigan, but teaching jobs here are hard to find right now."

"I know they are," Pat agreed with a sigh before offering, "Would she like me to keep an eye out for openings in the middle schools where we're working?"

"Yeah, I'm sure she would appreciate that," Randy said with a wink, the twinkle never leaving his eyes.

Pat smiled in satisfaction. By all appearances, Theresa was good for Randy. And, of course, all her sons deserved special loves in their lives.

The two continued shopping in a couple of more stores, finding good deals on a few shirts and on another pair of jeans.

Pat also found some pink and green accessories and a tulle mosquito net piece. She was redecorating Kevin's old room later in the summer, planning to make it ultra-feminine with lots of pink. She was planning for hat boxes filled with photos, handmade crafts, and cards from her sons when they were little, and she had even unpacked some of her old doll collection to put on display. She was also working on framing some photos of Suezell and her when they were little girls.

Pat could picture the room in her mind, and it made her smile. It would be a tribute to the golden memories of growing up a little girl.

"Do you want to grab some lunch, now?" Pat asked.

"Sure. Where do you want to eat?"

"Well, it's your birthday," Pat replied. "You pick the place."

"How about Red Lobster?" Randy suggested.

"Sounds good to me," Pat said as the two headed in the direction of the restaurant. "Don't let me forget to give you the rolls and some other food I brought with me. They're in my car."

Randy loved breads, though he almost never ate sweets, and she could predict that he would order steak and shrimp for lunch. Pat had to smile at life's little predictabilities. Randy and Kevin almost always choose the steak and shrimp combo when the family went out to eat.

The lunch hour rush was just ending, so they were seated right away. As predicted, Randy chose shrimp and steak and began digging into the cheesy biscuits the waitress had delivered. Pat decided to have the stuffed flounder. She loved fish, but usually only had it out of the home. She didn't appreciate the fishy smell it left in her house.

"Well, we found some good stuff today, didn't we?" Randy said with a smile.

"We have!" Pat agreed. "But maybe before we leave we can find a black bath mat and another mirror for your house."

"That would be great," Randy said, before adding, "Oh, and I still don't have my tuxedo shirt for the wedding."

"Oh my gosh!" Pat said, glancing up in surprise at his announcement. "Well, we have to get that today, too—only two weeks left until the big day!"

"Yeah, I guess we better," he nodded. "I still can't believe

Kevin's getting married. He seems so young, doesn't he?"

"It does seem that way to me, too," Pat said with an affectionate smile. "But then, I remember that I wasn't quite twenty-two when your Dad and I were married."

Randy was quiet for a moment.

"That sure worked out, didn't it, Mom?" he said finally. "So Kevin is probably fine. I just know I'm not ready to do that yet. There are just other things I have to take care of first, you know?"

Pat smiled at her son. She knew all too well that Palmer men did things in their own time.

A couple of hours passed, and the pair had managed to find everything on their list, even the tuxedo shirt. They headed to Pat's minivan to retrieve the rolls, crackers, and paper products for Randy, and then carried them to his car.

Pat smiled again at her son's taste as they loaded his car: he had driven his restored '74 Grandville, a classic red convertible, the length of a small boat, but Randy loved it, and Pat had to admit, it was a pretty sharp car.

Randy hugged her as the two realized the hour was getting late.

"I love you, Mom," he said, giving her a peck on the cheek. "And thanks for all the clothes and stuff for my house."

"I am glad to do it," Pat replied, squeezing his hand. "It was good to be with you today. I love you, too, Randy."

The late afternoon sun behind her, Pat began the drive back to St. Louis, her thoughts turning back to Randy. They had nearly lost him almost four years before in a horrible car accident. God had spared his life that terrible day, and Pat wondered if Randy was just beginning to appreciate what that had meant. She herself had been so frightened that night and for the next three days until he regained consciousness.

In many ways, Pat reflected, they were getting their Randy back after that ordeal. He had gone through some rocky times in his late teens and early twenties—not uncommon perhaps, but still nerve-wracking for loving, concerned parents.

Randy has certainly received his fair share of my prayer time! Pat thought with a smile.

Randy was, at his core, a gentle person with a funny, dry sense of humor—not to mention, he was loved by God, his family, and, of course, his Mom.

As any mother would, Pat found herself wanting to prod more about his relationship with Theresa. Where was their relationship heading? Was it a blossoming friendship? Or were they falling in love?

Oh, Pat knew Randy wasn't ready to settle down just yet, but when summer afternoons like this one were soft, warm and golden, it took her back in time to another summer—the summer of 1971 and the best summer of her life.

It had been a summer of bliss, of being happily in love—something Pat wished everyone in the world could experience.

Pat smiled as the clock of time seemed to rewind in her memory. *Everyone* should have a summer of '71.

CHAPTER NINE
Summer of 1971

Sometimes life surprises you. Sometimes things align in perfect harmony with every hope and fantasy you could've imagined, every sunset seems magical, every star shoots across a vast night sky just for couples in love. The world is opening up to endless possibilities of 'happily ever after,' and the man of your dreams is falling head over heels in love with you!

Pat had to admit that Suezell had been remarkably patient with her sister's endless mooning over the wonders of Jim Palmer. Of course, Pat suspected that perhaps it also had something to do with the fact that Suezell was pretty giddy over a guy she was dating herself.

Still, as much as Pat wanted to hear every detail of Suezell's unfolding fairytale, it seemed all Pat could do was daydream about Jim Palmer. She had been floating in an unending fantasy since their date the week before, and it made it difficult to focus on anything else. Her evenings were filled with talking nonstop about Jim to Suezell, her mom, Debbie—*anyone* who was willing to listen.

During the day, she kept busy with schoolwork, taking a three-week sociology course in order to graduate a semester early in December of that same year. Class met every day for five hours, but Pat didn't mind. She was enjoying the class. The lectures were mindless note-taking, and the tests were all essays, playing to one of her strengths as a student. She was earning an "A" in the class—

although during much of the lecture time, Pat grew starry-eyed and her thoughts strayed to the dreamy date with Jim Palmer.

"Oh, Deb," Pat sighed dreamily for what may have been the hundredth time as they drove home from class one afternoon. "It's not that he's perfect or anything like that... It's just that he's perfect *for me*! And did I tell you what he said before we said goodnight that night?"

Debbie giggled.

"Yes, you have," she responded, smiling affectionately. "But only five times—I'm definitely up for making it six!"

Pat threw her head back and laughed.

In later years, an older, wiser Pat would realize how that summer must've been for poor Debbie. Pat was, after all, displaying all of the classic behaviors of how a girl newly-in-love treats her best friend. But Debbie usually didn't seem to mind *too* much...

"Okay, Deb," Pat said, lowering her voice conspiratorly as she slowed her car in front of a farmhouse surrounded by pink petunias. "That's it! That's where he lives..."

"What?" Debbie stammered, suddenly realizing they were miles out of their way and shrinking down into her seat in horror. "What if he sees us!?"

"It's okay," Pat reassured her friend, laughing as she sped up again. "He's out of town this afternoon, and his family won't recognize this car."

As the farmhouse disappeared in her rearview mirror, Pat leaned back in her seat, letting the late afternoon sunshine bathe her face in warmth as she guided the car back toward the Oswald house. The car windows were down, and a soft breeze caressed her face tenderly, seemingly reminding her of life's little pleasures.

Now that class was over, Pat dropped Debbie off each day and spent her afternoons at home, helping pick green beans, snipping strawberries, and folding loads of laundry—all blissfully mindless tasks that left plenty of room for daydreaming.

The drive back to the Oswald farm was short, but Pat couldn't resist humming a song that seemed to always be on her mind these days.

"Oh, no!" Debbie groaned. "Not that song again! Seriously, Pat, how about we listen to the radio—please?"

Pat laughed. "Someone" by Ray Conniff and his orchestra played over and over again in her head as many times as she played the warped album she'd purchased at a fire sale earlier that spring. The lilting ballad had never made it to the top of the charts, and Pat felt like the only person in the world who loved the song; but she didn't care: the lyrics said it all. Jim *was* an answer to her prayers, and she had never imagined that love could be this wonderful.

To anyone observing my life from the outside, I probably seemed completely naïve, idealistic, carefree, and very, very young . . . But I wouldn't trade that blissful summer for a thousand others . . .

"Hi, Pat!" Jim was smiling warmly at her from the front porch.

"Jim, hi!" Pat responded brightly, opening the front door and waving him inside. "I'll be ready to go in a minute—I just need to grab a jacket."

"I'll wait," was his simple reply.

My heart caught in my throat, those words ripe with meaning. It seemed that all I had done was wait, and now, here we were, my dreams and fantasies coming true. We had waited long enough, and our time was now . . . this magical summer was simply meant to be . . .

It was a beautiful Saturday evening, and the pair found themselves once again at the Skytop Theater. Finding a spot near the back of the lot, Jim put the car into 'park,' before turning to Pat with a smile. Pat felt herself freeze as she flushed in anticipation, wishing more than anything in the world that Jim Palmer would simply pull her into his arms and kiss her for hours. She moved closer to him, barely able to resist herself.

Then, Pat smiled at Jim.

A grin spread across his face, and he cleared his throat, shifting almost nervously in his seat. He opened his mouth to say something, but seemed to think the better of it.

A moment of comfortable silence filled the car, as Pat realized that they both were thinking the same thoughts.

I held my breath, unable to believe the conflicting thoughts racing through my mind. I'd waited so long for a moment like this with Jim, and yet there was something almost mystical about it—precious and frail—as if giving in to even harmless, innocent passions would mar something truly beautiful that was unfolding . . .

"So, how was your week?" he suddenly asked, breaking the silence.

Pat grinned. What was it about this man that made her light-headed with desire one minute and then feel as if she were enjoying a comfortable conversation with a close girlfriend the next?

The two spent the entire evening talking, barely pausing for breath without even acknowledging whatever film happened to be rolling on the screen.

I can say anything to him, she marveled. *And he actually seems to like talking to me!*

Pat, always inquisitive about the lives of people around her, asked Jim questions about his family, his prospects for a teaching job, and farming—although not much of a farmer herself, she had certainly picked up the lingo after twenty years of living it and secretly hoped he was impressed. She inquired about his choice of a major, teaching mechanical and architectural drafting; how had his student-teaching gone?

Pat studied his face closely as she listened to his responses. There really was *something* about him—something special, secure, safe, genuine. And just when Pat Oswald wouldn't have thought she could be more in love, her heart fell just a little bit deeper for the wonderful man sitting next to her. It was the way his eyes lit when he talked about his work, the tenderness that colored his voice when he spoke of his family, the huskiness that his voice took on each time his eyes seemed to drink her in . . .

"Pat? Did you hear what I said?"

Pat flushed as she suddenly realized that she'd been openly staring at Jim and had been completely unaware that he was asking her a question.

"Um—I'm sorry. What did you say?" Pat asked reddening, grateful for the dimly-lit car.

Jim laughed.

Oh, how I love that laugh!

"I was asking about your family," he replied, his eyes twinkling with amusement.

The conversation continued. He asked about her goals, her friends, her hopes for the future. The pair sat close together in the roomy 1963 Dodge, previously passed down to Jim after being the family car for a number of years.

Somehow, some way, in the course of their conversation, Jim had put his arm around her. Pat couldn't hide the smile that spread across her face as a strange combination of electrical sparks and comforting warmth seared her spine at his touch. She felt safe and desirable all at once, and the anticipation that shot through her veins as he placed his hand on her knee was almost more than she could bear . . .

It was the most comfortable thing in the world—sitting in that car, albeit quite innocently, with Jim, and it was simultaneously the most extraordinary experience of my twenty years of existence—a strange blend of newfound desire and nervous butterflies . . .

"Hey," Jim suddenly exclaimed, turning up the radio. "Have you heard this song?"

Pat shook her head, but listened to the words of Delaney and Bonnie's "Never Ending Song of Love" with a smile spreading across her face.

"I really like this song," Jim said softly, looking into her eyes. "I think it says it all."

Pat felt herself flush.

The evening ended all too soon, but Pat, learning her near-disastrous lesson from the last date, was prepared to linger a bit longer this time as Jim walked her to the door. While he didn't linger long, he asked her for a date the following Monday. It would be Memorial Day, only two days away.

The world couldn't have been more perfect.

I don't know that I have the words to describe how I felt that weekend, waiting until the next moment I would spend time with Jim Palmer.

My head was spinning, and I felt as though I was floating through the hours. I tried to focus on reading for my class, I tried to focus on daily chores at hand, diligently cleaning the house over and over again until my mother began teasing me that she just might fall in love with Jim, too—out of gratitude!

Memorial Day dawned warm and bright, and the Oswald family gathered at the St. Louis cemetery to lay flowers on the grave of Pat's grandmother, as well as on her brother Tom's grave. Pat spent the rest of the day studying and helping with chores around the farmhouse. She often did the baking for her family, and so today, she spent the afternoon in the kitchen, baking blondies, a batch of yeast rolls, and pie crusts that she would fill with butterscotch and coconut cream later on in the week.

As evening approached, the butterflies returned to Pat's stomach, and she found herself a little breathless as she dressed in a red and white striped skirt with a red, sleeveless knit top. Easing her feet into white shoes, she surveyed her appearance in the mirror, critically examining every invisible flaw until she was satisfied at last.

And then, from downstairs, there was a knock at the door.

"Pat?" her mother called up the stairs nonchalantly. "Jim Palmer is here."

Pat drew a steadying breath and descended the stairs to find Jim chatting easily with her parents in the entryway.

Romaine and Naomi had met Jim at the winter party, and, of course, they had heard countless hours of stories from a lovesick Pat. Fortunately for Pat, though, the conversation wasn't centered on their daughter's giddy romantic fantasies; Jim and Romaine were talking about farming.

"So, you farm with your dad and brothers right, Jim?" Romaine was asking.

"That's right," Jim confirmed with a nod. "We have a farm north of town on Chippewa Road."

Romaine snapped his fingers in recollection.

"You know, I think I have seen your dad at FFA meetings," he said. "Do you have your crops all in?"

Jim nodded.

"We could really use a rain though," he said, shaking his head in concern. "The corn and soybeans could use the boost."

"Yeah, a little rain could make a real difference," Romaine agreed heartily.

At that moment, Naomi caught the pleading look in her daughter's eye.

"Well, you kids have fun," Naomi cut in, breezily ending the farm talk and opening the back door so the pair could head out into their evening.

Pat flashed her mother a grateful smile as she followed Jim outside.

Once they were in the car, Jim was silent until he turned the key in the ignition. As the car roared to life, he paused for a moment and turned to look at her.

"You look really nice tonight, Pat," he said with a shy smile.

Pat's heart was racing.

"Thank you!" she murmured as she blushed.

The moment was heavy with silence and unspoken desire. Her gaze met his, and their eyes locked.

Pat smiled.

Jim grinned at her, a thousand thoughts racing through his mind all at once as they sat there close together. Then, he cleared his throat.

"Would you like to go bowling tonight?" he asked, breaking the spell before he let himself go too far.

"Sure, that sounds like fun," she said with a shaky laugh.

Was it only seconds before that we were locked in a passion-filled moment, struggling to regain control of our emotions and longing? Pat thought, still reeling a bit from the smoldering look in his eyes a moment before. *And now, here we are, laughing and chatting like old friends. It really is too wonderful to be making this up . . .*

"You understand that I'm not a great bowler, right?" she added tentatively.

He laughed.

"That's okay," he assured her. "I took it in college, but I am far from an accomplished bowler myself."

"Okay, then let's go for it," Pat said enthusiastically.

He's so amazing, and he's okay with a girl like me who's completely clueless about sports? Thank you again, God . . . Jim Palmer really is a dream come true . . .

The pair laughed at their gutter balls and cheered each other on when they were lucky enough to roll a strike or a spare. Jim grinned sheepishly as the final score revealed him to be the winner. Pat just beamed happily at him. She didn't care that she had lost the game. She, in fact, knew that she had won. The only thing that mattered in the world was that she was with the man of her dreams.

As the evening continued, I realized that I was falling a little more for Jim Palmer each moment we spent together. I loved talking with him, getting to know more of who he really was. I genuinely enjoyed the man I was coming to know: he was serious about things that really mattered, thoughtful, so polite—always holding doors for me, the perfect gentleman even in moments that I wished he would take me into his arms and kiss me until I couldn't see clearly.

And it was amazing and wonderful—he seemed to be falling for me, too . . .

The full moon was high in a velvety blue sky when Jim walked Pat to the door of her parents' home later that evening. Pat's heart was racing at the very nearness of him walking beside her. They reached the back door, and Jim reached out and squeezed her hand.

"Well," he said somewhat shyly. "Goodnight, Pat Oswald!"

Pat stood for a moment, completely frozen, a thousand thoughts racing through her mind, as he started to walk away.

"Um, Jim?" she called after him.

Jim paused on the steps and half turned back, looking at her expectantly.

"Yeah?"

Pat knew she would never know what gave her the courage to rush over to where he stood, gently planting a kiss on his cheek.

"I had a really good time, too," she said breathlessly smiling into his eyes, their faces inches apart. "Thank you!"

Jim smiled tenderly and put his arms around her. Pat was sure she couldn't breathe in that moment as he kissed her lips, gently at first then with growing intensity.

They held each other for a moment, savoring the magic of a first kiss until Jim spoke.

"Would you like to go with me to Montrose on Thursday?" he asked. "I have a teaching interview, and I thought if you wanted to, you could ride along with me."

Pat smiled warmly at him, feeling a little weak in the knees as she stood with his arms encircling her. "Sure, I would love to!" she replied, her breath catching in her throat as the moonlight caught his face. "What time is your interview?"

"It's at two o'clock," Jim responded, distractedly clearing his throat, seemingly trying to remind himself of a gentleman's self-control, yet so unwilling to let her go. "So we probably need to leave by 12:30—I want to be sure to arrive early."

So like him, Pat thought with an affectionate smile.

"That sounds great," she replied as Jim reluctantly released her from his embrace. He turned to continue down the steps, pausing a moment to take her in once more.

"Goodnight, Pat," Jim said, his voice husky with emotion.

"Goodnight, Jim," she replied softly. "See you Thursday!"

I accompanied him on many trips that summer, loving every moment of becoming a part of the life of this wonderful man. Of course, it was an added bonus that he was going through the same job search that I would be doing in a few months! I loved discussing how his interviews had gone, and I loved that we shared the same career choice—it was important to me to be sharing that with Jim.

Jim had questions for me, too, mainly about my faith. Faith and prayer had been a part of my life since becoming a believer nearly two years earlier. It was a very personal relationship with the Creator of the Universe, and now it seemed that God was bringing Jim into that bond as well.

Jim had confided in me that his family had never attended church during his childhood, and he said he didn't really know a lot about God. But he wanted to. He asked me thought-provoking questions about what I believed and why, and I loved that it was yet another thing we could share. That was truly very important to me as well . . . In fact, it meant everything . . .

It was as if God Himself had designed that magical summer just for us. Everything was aligning perfectly . . .

It was late June when Pat invited Jim to visit her church one Sunday morning, and he accepted. She felt a surge of pride walking into the white-steepled building hand-in-hand with such an amazing, handsome man.

As the service commenced, Jim seemed to be enjoying himself, and he was listening intently. Pat's church was known for being friendly, and after the service, everyone greeted him warmly. He grinned at each greeting, clearly at ease.

One sunny afternoon, the two were enjoying a moment of quiet, sitting under a shady elm tree in Pat's backyard sipping iced tea.

"It really is brilliant," Jim's voice broke the silence.

Pat turned her head to look at him quizzically.

"What is?" she asked with a smile.

"This," Jim said, holding up a blade of grass between his fingers. "The design is simply brilliant! I mean, it's functional, aesthetic . . . "

Pat chuckled.

"Spoken like a true engineer," she teased, lacing her fingers through his.

Jim grinned before turning thoughtful again.

"God *is* brilliant," he said softly, looking up at the sky. "And He created everything and still has time for people? He even brought us together! That's pretty amazing, too, don't you think?"

Pat smiled again.

"I do," was her simple reply.

"You know," Jim said turning back to Pat. "Your faith always seems to make you so happy. You really do have a positive outlook on life all of the time."

Pat smiled tenderly at Jim as he continued.

"You know," he said quietly, squeezing her hand. "You're my Angel, Pat. You're a messenger who helped me to know God. And I will always be grateful for that."

From that day forward, Jim never called me anything but "Angel."

June turned to July, and the couple continued to spend most of their time together. One afternoon, Jim invited Pat to his parents' home to meet them, along with his younger brother, Ted.

"Why, you must be Pat!" Jim's dad, Leslie, enthusiastically greeted Pat, pulling her into a hug. "It's so nice to finally meet you! We've heard so much about you."

Pat smiled shyly, slowly relaxing as introductions were made. Jim's mother, Ida Mae, squeezed her hand and smiled warmly.

"It's so very nice to have you here," she said quietly, holding out a platter of fresh warm cookies as they all made themselves comfortable in the living room. "I've been so anxious to get to know the girl who's occupying my son's thoughts!"

"Hey, Jimmy-boy!" a voice echoed in the hallway as the back door slammed.

Jim's brother, Ted, grinned as he bounded into the living room, tousling his older brother's hair before flopping down onto the sofa. Jim laughed and affectionately tweaked his brother's ear.

"Teddy," Jim said, putting his arm around Pat's shoulders. "This is Pat."

"Hiya, Pat!" Ted responded with a grin, shaking her hand enthusiastically. "It's nice to finally have the 'lovebirds' here! We were starting to think Jim had made you up!"

Lovebirds . . . It described us perfectly. Every time I was near him, I could barely hear anything above the beating of my pounding heart . . . I was falling in love, and the euphoric bliss was unlike anything I'd ever known . . .

By the end of July, Jim had decided to accept a teaching position in Millington, almost two hours to the east of St. Louis. Ida Mae didn't attempt to hide her disappointment, quietly urging Pat to talk him into accepting a teaching position closer to home. Pat, however, knew Jim wanted to teach drafting rather than metal or woodshop and could only do that in a school farther away, so she didn't try to intervene.

Pat would, of course, have preferred that Jim live closer. The future felt a little uncertain. She would be living at home that fall, student teaching at a local school, but she also knew that the first teaching position was an important choice, and Pat didn't know where she would be teaching come January.

With teaching contract in hand, Jim invited his parents to help him look for housing. Not finding much available for rent in the small Millington community, he decided to buy a 12x50 mobile home, completely decked out in the color of early '70's: harvest gold appliances, gold shag carpeting, even a gold-flowered wallboard in the kitchen. It was perfect choice for a young bachelor, and he kept it neat and clean.

Crickets were chirping noisily and a warm breeze ruffled Pat's hair as she sat on the front porch steps, anticipation stirring the butterflies in her stomach. A car pulled up, and she heard a car door.

"Hi, Angel!" a voice echoed from the driveway.

"Hi, Honey!" she responded, jumping up and pulling Jim into

her arms.

Their lips met in a kiss, and Pat felt a shiver travel up her spine.

"I missed you!" she murmured, nuzzling his neck.

"It's only been a couple of days, Angel," he chuckled softly. "But if this is the 'welcome home' I get, I'll go away more often!"

He pulled her into another kiss, their passion growing as she felt his arms tighten around her.

"I am so lucky to have you to hold," he whispered into her hair. "You are so special, Angel!"

"Oh, Honey," Pat sighed breathlessly between kisses. "*You are special for so many reasons! You're sincere and modest—so unlike any guy I've ever known!*"

"You think things through, make good decisions," Pat continued. "And you make sure things get done . . . after all, first things first."

Pat smiled into his eyes lovingly, and Jim looked genuinely surprised.

"What is it?" Pat questioned at the look in his eyes.

"Well," he said thoughtfully. "You really do know *me* . . ."

Jim was silent for a moment.

"I have something to tell you," he said softly.

Jim traced his fingers down her cheek and smiled tenderly.

"I love you, Angel."

Jim Palmer said 'I love you' multiple times every day from that day forward, but I will never, ever forget that moment. It wasn't a phrase he used lightly. It was a carefully thought-out, sincere declaration of his feelings for me, a 'never ending love,' just like the song that he loved so much. I knew in that moment more than ever that he was the man I wanted to spend the rest of my life with . . .

The magical summer of '71 continued with picnics to towering forests of Hartwick Pines in Northern Michigan. Beneath the enormous virgin pines, they held each other and kissed before feasting on Pat's homemade lunches: fried chicken, potato salad, rolls, topped off with Jim's favorite, peach pie.

The couple spent some Saturdays at her parents' cottage on the sparkling waters of Higgins Lake, taking long walks, playing in the water, sunbathing on the beach and basking in the sunshine of true love.

Pat hummed "Someone," smiled and sighed blissfully, and daydreamed about her future with Jim Palmer. The sky was brilliant blue, trees were vibrant green, flowers bloomed as never before . . . life was so good . . .

CHAPTER TEN
Girls Day Out

Love arrives in all kinds of ways—often when it is least expected. Sometimes it is a slowly-evolving recognition that this is the person you want to spend the rest of your life with. Other times, the recognition of your mate is instant and intense.

For some, love is life-changing, causing upheaval and chaos. For others, love seems to ease comfortably into your life, bringing with it the most subtle adjustments. Some lovers are energized and appear to come alive in a relationship; still others find themselves calmed and settled by this thing called love.

Some relationships demand a great deal of hard work—lots of compromises and adjustments. I also knew from personal experience that for a few people, love is easy and flows as naturally and unhindered as a babbling brook in springtime...

Pat had always been fascinated with "how did you meet your mate" stories. It was one of her favorite parts of the classic film, "When Harry Met Sally"—all of the elderly couples sharing their unique stories of lasting love and how it all began.

Many years later, as an adult, Pat and her best friend, Karen, were always discussing and analyzing relationships. They joked that they liked to think of themselves as "social-psychologists," pondering the ever-mysterious depths and eternal twists and turns of human relationships. They spent hours discussing why certain relationships worked or didn't work, and how various individuals completed their spouses and balanced their lives.

Of course, as a mother, Pat was always the most interested in her sons' relationships, keeping an ever-watchful eye without prying *too* much into their private lives. She did, however, pride herself on being a match-maker, whether it was for her co-workers or even her own sons, as had been the case with Matt and Heidi.

Kevin and Andrea had met without Pat's help.

Although she was pretty reluctant to admit that it was even possible for her boys to meet their true loves without any involvement from her *at all*, Pat knew that Kevin had found a gem when he met Andrea.

Kevin and Andrea were both freshmen at Calvin College in Grand Rapids, and Andrea had actually initially been interested in Kevin's roommate at the time. That romance had been brief and uneventful. The following July, however, Andrea had called Kevin, and they started casually talking on the phone from time to time.

Eventually, Andrea pointedly told him she would very much like to drive to St. Louis to see him—just to get away for the day. They had spent the entire day at the house, discussing mutual friends from Calvin, comparing the ups and downs of what each was doing for a summer job, and imagining how their second year of college might go. A few weeks later, it became clear that romance was in the air, and the pair began dating.

Nearly three years later, the day after their college graduation, Kevin was spending the night with Andrea's family. He went to Andrea's room early the next morning to wake her up for devotions . . . and it was then that he proposed to her.

With Kevin and Andrea's wedding less than two weeks away, Heidi had hatched a plan for the Palmer women to "join forces" and spend a luxurious day at the spa.

"After all, Mom," Heidi had said when they'd spoken on the phone the week before. "I remember that the last couple of weeks before my wedding were insane, so Andrea could probably really use this right about now!"

It was typical of Heidi, thoughtful to the core and fully aware of how important a day like this one could be for the three of them to share.

So, Heidi had made appointments for them all at a spa in Lansing where Andrea, Pat, and she would meet at ten a.m. to begin a day of pampering, conversation, and bonding between mother-in-law and daughters-in-law.

Pat was keenly aware that having daughters-in-law would never be the same as having a daughter of her own—the roles were simply different. But, more than anything, she tried hard to be a great mother-in-law. She herself had been blessed with a wonderful mother-in-law and had missed her terribly in the decade since she passed away.

Ida Mae, like herself, had never had her own daughter, and yet she had always been warm and loving to Pat. She had also served as a role model for her, both as a mother-in-law and a grandmother.

Pat smiled, grateful for the opportunity to spend time with Heidi and Andrea and so honored that they had chosen to include her in their lives. They were both smart and beautiful women—joys to have in the family.

Pat wondered, too, if perhaps, they both realized that forging a good relationship with their mother-in-law was beneficial for their marriages, especially since the Palmer family had always been so close.

In any case, Pat found herself hoping it wasn't out of some sense of obligation or fear that they had invited her along today. She didn't think so. Each girl had invited her to join in the search for the perfect wedding dress.

Still, she felt certain that both of her sons had suggested those invitations. Matt and Kevin knew their Mom's love of shopping and clothes and knew she had always missed out on the chance of shopping with a daughter.

Pushing her worries aside, Pat decided to assume only the best intentions and just enjoy their day together. It had, after all, been a sweet gesture to include her in this special event.

Pat tuned her radio to her favorite 'Oldies' station and found herself relaxing as she began the fifty-minute drive to Lansing. Andrea was out of school for the summer, and Heidi had a few days off between her residency and her new work at the clinic. Pat herself was once again grateful for the flexibility of her work. Today would be a day of fun indulgence.

The three women were arriving separately because each had evening commitments in different areas of the state. Pat was really looking forward to seeing the two girls and had brought along a pair of earrings she'd picked out for each of them. She knew how much they both loved jewelry and congratulated herself on selecting wisely for each of them.

Heidi's were simple and small, silver earrings designed in a series of hoops and beads. Pat had reasoned they would go well with several outfits and were perfect for a variety of situations—even at the Clinic where Heidi would be working as a Doctor of Internal Medicine in a few more weeks.

Pat was proud of Heidi. She had worked very hard to complete medical school and three years of residency; soon, all of that would be behind her, and she could begin her life's passion once and for all. The earrings, Pat realized as she hummed along to a tune on the radio, reflected Heidi: she was practical and hardworking, but she was also enthusiastic, fun-loving, and had a laugh that was contagious.

Heidi and Pat shared a lot of the same interests, too. They both, for example, were addicted to tableware, dinner napkins and napkins rings, china, and dishes of all sorts. Heidi had also taken up quilting and was becoming an accomplished quilter. Pat had not mastered it, but her own mother had. Pat often wondered if it might become a hobby in her retirement—not that that was likely to happen any time soon!

Andrea's earrings were also selected especially for her. They were bright blue beaded chandeliers. Andrea's bridesmaid dresses were royal blue, and she looked great in bright colors like reds, blues, white, and pinks. Pat felt certain that the earrings would be perfect in her new daughter-in-law's wardrobe as a high school Spanish teacher.

Andrea and Heidi were, in many ways, quite different from one another—but then, Pat reasoned, so were Matt and Kevin. Andrea was the third in a family of four children, the oldest girl with a younger sister—the same as Pat.

Both Heidi and Andrea were intelligent, hardworking girls who had been privileged to grow up in loving Christian families. Andrea, however, had spent much of her early life on the mission field in Honduras and Puerto Rico. While that life had certainly been exciting, unique, and rewarding, Pat sensed that Andrea was anxious to have a home and raise a family in one place. Andrea had even once confided to her that she was a little jealous of the fact that Kevin had friends in the wedding who had been friends of his since second grade. For Andrea, that had simply not been a part of her life.

Andrea was quieter than both Pat and Heidi. She was pleasant, friendly, and open—just not as emotional or effusive as the other Palmer women. Andrea was confident and certain of her decisions, though—much more confident than Pat had been at that point in her own life.

And Pat knew that Andrea was certain of her love for Kevin, and that was all she wanted for her son—the love of a Godly woman. Pat also recognized that Kevin, true to form, contributed emotion, enthusiasm, and laughter to their relationship. They were a match made in Heaven, and each gave the other what they needed to be complete.

Just like every good relationship should be, Pat reflected wistfully.

It wasn't long before Pat found parking close by the spa and turned her car off just as Heidi arrived. Moments later, the two spotted Andrea pulling into the same city parking lot.

Pat smiled as their excitement for the upcoming pampering bubbled over. She knew that while neither of the girls had been the least bit deprived as children, neither of them had been privileged to the point of spoiling. Today was indeed a treat for all three of them. They entered the spa amid giggles and chit-chat about how great massages, manicures, and facials were going to be.

"So, what are we having done today?" Pat asked as a hostess seated them and handed them clipboards with some paperwork to fill out.

Heidi's eyes were sparkling as her enthusiasm reached a fever pitch.

"Well, first, each of us is going to have a one-hour full-body massage!" she grinned. "I've been on my feet a lot the last few days, and this is going to feel great—oh, and I'm sure the two of you won't mind it *too much* either . . . "

Andrea nodded with a chuckle.

"Oh, I think a massage is exactly what I need to just relax and do *anything but* think about wedding planning," Andrea sighed quietly. "I *loved* finding the dress, but since then? Well, it has pretty much stopped being much fun!"

"Well then, a massage is just what all three of us need," Pat concluded. "I really do enjoy them, but it's kind of a guilty pleasure that I don't allow myself too often."

"Good!" Heidi exclaimed, delighted at their reaction to the plan she'd set in motion. "Ah, I just love that soothing music and those amazing lotions! I can hardly wait even five more minutes!"

"Well, I've never had a massage," Andrea confessed with a small smile. "But my friends tell me they are to die for—so I can't wait!"

The hostess appeared again, collecting the clipboards and

exchanging them for mugs of steaming herbal tea. Heidi took a sip, inhaling deeply, before turning to Andrea.

"So, Andrea, are you pretty much all set for the wedding and reception?" she asked.

"I think so," Andrea replied. "We have the string quartet confirmed for the service, and my sister-in-law is looking at music for her solos. The girls' dresses are all altered, and I reviewed the flower order with the florist yesterday. I just didn't realize how many decisions there are to make—tons of little details. Okay, so I have to know—did you panic before your wedding, Heidi?"

Heidi laughed.

"Well, define 'panic'!" she chuckled before turning serious. "No, not really, but it *was* a crazy busy time: I had just graduated from med school, and Matt was busy with his landscape work. He was a huge help with making arrangements—I *hate* to make phone calls, so he did lots of the confirmation calls for me."

"I'm afraid Kevin is a little last minute," Andrea confessed a little sheepishly. "He still has to choose music for the reception, buy groomsmen gifts, and lots of other stuff. He *did* reserve the convertible we are driving to the airport—so at least *that's* done—oh, and I think he has the honeymoon reservations confirmed."

"Guys usually take care of the honeymoon, don't they?" Heidi asked with a smile. "How about you, Mom? Your marriage is such a legend—what was the planning like for your wedding?"

A smile spread across Pat's face as she was tempted to drift back into a host of beautiful memories.

"Oh, weddings in the early '70's were pretty simple," Pat laughed, determined to stay focused on the present. "It was a church ceremony with just cake and punch at the reception—and that probably lasted all of an hour!"

"Weddings should be fun, though," she continued. "And I think today's ceremonies are just beautiful. Of course, the wedding's not the most important thing—*marriages* are what make up the best part of our lives, those are the moments that really matter in the end."

"So, you're going to Mexico on your honeymoon, right, Andrea?" Pat asked, shifting the subject back to the girls.

"That's right," Andrea replied, excitement filling her voice. "It'll be a short trip because Kevin is in a friend's wedding the week after ours, but it will be fun to just lie on the beach for a few days. Matt and you went to Hawaii on yours, didn't you, Heidi?"

"Oh yeah," Heidi grinned. "And I would do it again in a heartbeat!"

"Excuse me, Ladies," the hostess apologetically interrupted. "But we're ready for you now!"

Moments later, Pat undressed in the dimly-lit room and laid down on the massage table, the soft music soothing her and drawing her mind into the past. She closed her eyes and, even before the massage began, she found herself far, far away. Once again, it was 1971 when magic and romance filled her every moment . . .

Summer warmth gave way to cooler autumn days, and I often wondered if my magical fairytale would end. Was it too good to be true? Would the clock strike midnight on Cinderella's dream? Would my life suddenly go back to the way it had always been before Jim, void of all color and magic?

Jim had begun his first year of teaching at a small high school some sixty miles away, while I lived with my parents, student-teaching at a high school nearby. But as autumn colors blossomed onto the Mid-Michigan landscape, our romance did, too . . . The only distance between us was geographical.

It had been two years since the autumn afternoon that I had first seen him in Wightman Hall on the campus of CMU. The world was once again vibrant with color and aglow with the bliss and magic of new love.

I sent him silly "I love you" cards daily and could barely stand the wait for the coming weekend when I would see his smile again. He wrote me letters nearly every night, always addressing them to "Angel" and always filling them with messages of love.

Yet all the while we were distracted by thoughts of one another, we were, as always, mature, practical, and focused on our beloved teaching careers. Balance was important to us—as important as our drive to be successful.

Winter came, and, with it, my college graduation day. As I walked in my cap and gown, I could see Jim in the sea of faces, cheering loudly and beaming with pride. Later that evening after the well-wishes and congratulations from family and friends had quieted, he gave me a heart-shaped locket with a tiny pair of wedding rings adorning the face of it. There was talk of when we would marry . . . I felt a deep peace about my relationship with Jim, and the thought of a future together filled me with intense joy—a joy like none I'd ever known . . .

Dreaming of a future with Jim, but true to her pragmatic self, Pat began her search for a teaching position. It was nerve-wracking, to say the least, going through the process of interviews and callbacks. All she wanted in the world was to find a job and do it well.

It was halfway through the school year when she landed a home economics teaching position in Yale, Michigan. It was a small town near Lake Huron, less than thirty minutes from the Canadian border. She found a tiny log home in town and rented it for the semester. The home had one small bedroom, a tiny bath, and efficiency kitchen, but it suited her needs just perfectly. The feeling of independence was exhilarating, and it was a solid choice for her first real home.

It was strange to think of, but Pat suddenly felt like a "grown-up." The feeling of wealth when her first paycheck arrived was almost overwhelming. She had been on a very tight budget all through college, and a salary of over $7,000 a year seemed too good to be true. She walked through the local grocery store, smiling to herself as she surveyed the shelves stocked with treats.

I can buy whatever I want! she thought with satisfaction.

And she did. She had always craved store-bought items, a rare treat growing up in her parents' home, so Pat indulged, buying Twinkies, chips, lunch meats, candy, all kinds of foods—everything she knew was completely unhealthy, but nonetheless within her budget!

The next day after her stomachache subsided, she chided herself and marched herself down to the nearest department store to buy a sewing machine—a much more practical choice, very "Becky-Home-Eckey," as Jim teased her lovingly.

Being a first-year teacher was hard work. Pat worked diligently each night, preparing to teach clothing and textiles, foods and nutrition, child development, and interior design each day. But Tuesdays were saved for her Jim. Every Tuesday, he made the hour-drive to spend the evening in Pat's open arms.

It might've seemed old-fashioned to her friends, but she loved making dinner for the two of them, trying out new recipes and serving them by candlelight. Their evenings together were filled with tender embraces, long passionate kisses, and dreams of a lifetime spent together. Other nights, Jim worked long hours, grading dozens of student mechanical drafting assignments, but Tuesdays were for his "Angel."

"After all," he often said with a smile and a twinkle in his eye. "First things first!"

Jim asked me to marry him on April 1st of 1972, the same day a beautiful diamond ring he had ordered was ready to be picked up from a local jeweler. We had actually already set a wedding date and had started to make arrangements for a simple ceremony to take place the third weekend in June—so, the proposal wasn't exactly a surprise . . . but it was still one of the most wonderful moments of my life . . .

"So, how was your day, Angel?" Jim asked, his eyes never leaving the road in front of them as they made the drive to her parents' house for a relaxing evening of food and games.

"It was a long week," Pat said with a weary smile, twirling strands of Jim's hair through her fingers from the seat next to him. "But it was good—and none of the students played April Fools jokes on me today, so I'm thankful for that!"

Jim chuckled and grew silent. Pat tilted her head and watched him for a moment.

"Are you all right, Honey?" she asked, concern coloring her voice. "A long week for you, too?"

"Oh, I'm fine," he responded quietly, but Pat knew him better. *Something* was certainly on his mind. He was usually so attentive, and yet tonight he seemed a thousand miles away.

As if reading her thoughts, Jim reached down and squeezed her hand reassuredly.

"Angel," he said, seeming to choose his words carefully. "You know I love you, right?"

She smiled dreamily.

"I do!" she confirmed, confused as to where he was going with the conversation, but went along with it, adding, "And I love you, too, Honey!"

"We're both in a good place in our lives," he continued, his knuckles turning white as he gripped the steering wheel harder. "I mean, we've both accomplished what we set out to."

Pat nodded in the dimly-lit car, squeezing his hand affectionately, encouraging him to continue.

"I guess what I'm trying to say," he went on. "Is that you've changed my life—you know that, right?"

Pat smiled warmly at him as a thrill went through her body.

"Of course I do, and you've made me so happy, Jim!"

The car was silent for a moment, leaving Pat slightly puzzled. *Well, that was strange . . .*

Then, without warning, Jim suddenly guided the car to the side of the road, putting it into 'park,' as the motor idled quietly.

"Angel," he said, his voice rising in urgency as he shifted his body sideways in the front seat and grasped her hands in his. "There's something I have to ask you, and I can't wait any longer."

"Jim—"

The butterflies in Pat's stomach constricted her throat; she wasn't sure she could breathe in that moment.

"Angel," Jim's eyes grew tender as he cupped her face in his hands. "Will you marry me?"

It seemed that for a moment Heaven and Earth were suspended in time. I remember that I laughed in delight as tears of joy sprang to my eyes. The man of my dreams had just asked me to be his for all time. All he needed was an answer.

"YES!" Pat exclaimed, throwing her arms around his neck.

Looking back, it was a simple proposal—especially by today's standards ... There was no fancy dinner with a ring hidden inside a cake, no hot air balloon ride or message on a scoreboard ... but to me, it was the most ecstatic moment of my life.

It was official—I would be Mrs. Jim Palmer! The ring was beautiful—a white gold band with a small, round diamond encrusted in brushed gold.

I remember holding his face in my hands and staring into his eyes.

"I love you, Jim Palmer," Pat said, tears of joy filling her eyes.

He grinned at her.

"I love you more."

"Impossible," she countered, shaking her head.

"*Not* impossible," Jim murmured, trailing kisses up her cheek.

"A tie?" she asked, squeezing his hand.

"A tie," he agreed with a nod.

Moments later, the pair were on their way to the home where Suezell was babysitting for the night. Twenty minutes and a flurry of delighted hugs and tears later, they were headed back to Pat's parents' home.

Romaine wordlessly gripped Jim's hand firmly, attempting to hide his emotion of the moment. Tears filling her eyes, Naomi pulled her daughter into her embrace and whispered, "I hope you'll always be as happy as you are today!"

Pat smiled into her mother's shoulder.

We will!

Chapter Eleven
A Dance Partner

'I hope you'll always be as happy as you are today' . . . It was a prayer I breathed each and every day as Jim and I began planning our life together. The future was a golden, hazy horizon, alive with possibility and shrouded in love.

It seemed our lives were really beginning. We were beginning a graceful dance of life and love and the frailty that ensues . . . And every day, I marveled at how lucky I was to be dancing with Jim . . .

"Mom?"

Pat jolted from a dazed sleep, the mingling fragments of memories and dreams of 1972 still filling her mind with fog and confusion as she realized she was in the present once more.

"Are you still awake, Mom?" she heard Kevin whisper again.

Rousing herself from sleep, Pat sat up to see Kevin standing in her bedroom doorway.

"Absolutely," she said, stifling a yawn. "Let's go in the kitchen; I could use some tea."

Sleep suddenly didn't matter. It was only days before Kevin and Andrea's wedding, and she was anxious for a chance to talk with him.

She and Kevin had always shared a special bond, as do most mothers with their youngest child. As a child, Kevin had been the one to curl up next to her in the evenings and chatter on about his day, his favorite toy, even his thoughts on the world until he could barely keep his eyes open.

Now, however, late-night chats with him had become common for the past eight years or so—at least, when he was home from college—and far too often, it was Pat fighting to stay awake as the night grew older.

But late-night conversations were something between the two of them that she loved more than anything, and she wouldn't trade any of those moments for the world—especially tonight. It was likely that tonight's talk would be the last; after all, Kevin would be married and living with his wife in a few short days.

Married! His wife!

It still sounded so strange to connect the two phrases to the ever-happy-go-lucky, free-spirited Kevin! Pat could hardly believe that her baby was now an adult, soon to have a wife and home of his own. Wasn't it only yesterday that he was throwing tiny arms around her neck, whispering, 'I love you, Mommy'?

Time passes all too quickly when it comes to those we love . . .

Pat crawled from bed, lifted her robe from a nearby chair and followed Kevin into the kitchen.

"So, how did shopping for the groomsmen gifts go?" she asked, putting some water on to boil.

Kevin and Andrea had spent the evening in Lansing trying to find gifts for his best friend and his three older brothers. True to form, it was something Kevin simply 'hadn't gotten around to yet'—even though the wedding was merely days away.

Kevin was notorious for doing things at the last minute, never the most organized one in the family, Pat recalled. He was in sixth grade when he began his forgetful young adolescence, and it had been a running joke among his brothers that Kevin just might forget to show up to his own wedding—hopefully, this wouldn't be the case . . . although Pat found herself subtly mentioning the specific wedding date often in casual conversations with Kevin, along with phrases like 'a week from Saturday.'

Just in case, she smiled affectionately. *I mean, you just never know with Kevin . . .*

"It went pretty well," Kevin answered with a grin, interrupting her thoughts. "I had business card holders engraved for Matt and Jeff, and I bought Randy some cuff-links—you know him and jewelry—so, I think he will like them."

"And I picked up a copy of a special edition of C.S. Lewis for 'the other Jeff,'" Kevin added. "Lewis is his favorite author."

Pat chuckled. Kevin's best friend, Jeff, had always been referred to within the family as "the other Jeff" to avoid confusion between him and Kevin's big brother. The name had stuck over the years.

"Oh, that sounds just perfect for all of them," Pat replied, joining Kevin at the kitchen table, mug of tea in hand. "So, are you just about ready for the wedding?"

"I think so," Kevin responded, counting off items on his fingers. "I have the convertible rented to get us around, and the arrangements for the first night are all set. Then, we fly to Mexico early on Sunday morning."

Kevin paused for a moment, as if weighing his words carefully.

"How are *you* doing, Mom?" he asked, studying her closely. "Are you okay with everything?"

"Oh, I'm fine, Kevin," Pat reassured him with a warm smile. "I really am! It's just hard to let you go—I will really miss you!"

"Mom!" Kevin protested with a lighthearted laugh. "I am going to be living *just across the street* from you—less than a block away!"

Pat laughed. She had to admit he was right on that one.

"But I know it won't be the same," his voice softened with understanding. "You and I have always been pretty close . . . I am true-blue Momma's boy!"

Pat laughed again

"What do you mean by 'Momma's boy'?" she chuckled, sipping her tea and feeling the warmth fill her insides. "You guys are all so independent. I really don't take care of you much anymore or cater to your every wish—never have, in fact."

"Oh no, not like that," he replied, correcting himself. "I mean, you and I talk about lots of things, and I have a closer relationship with you than any of my friends do with their moms—*that's* what I meant!"

"And I wouldn't have it any other way," Pat smiled as her eyes grew a bit misty. "You know, I think guys who really love their moms make the best husbands—your dad always loved his mom."

Pat was quiet for a moment before adding, "How does Andrea feel about our relationship? I mean, some girls might have a hard time with their fiancé being so close to his mother."

"Oh, she's fine with it," Kevin replied, dismissing any worry with a wave of his hand. "She's pretty laid-back about stuff like that, and she thinks you're pretty great anyway."

"You know, Mom," Kevin continued. "It's weird. I've dated other girls—and maybe I could have been happy with one or two of them . . . *maybe*—but *Andrea* is the only one . . . well, the only one that I feel I can be 'one' with."

Pat smiled affectionately at her youngest son.

"That *is* important," she responded. "And you know I have always said that Andrea is a wonderful girl."

Kevin grinned in agreement.

"I think so, too!"

"And as close as you and I are, Kevin," Pat continued, taking on a serious tone. "I want you to know that if ever you are forced to choose between Andrea or me—you know, making one of us happy—always, *always*, choose Andrea. That's what marriage should be. No matter what, I will always love you."

Kevin smiled at her in understanding, then suddenly jumped

to his feet.

"Come on, Mom," he said, his eyes twinkling. "Let's practice our Mother and Groom dance!"

"What, *now*?" Pat asked, throwing her head back and laughing. "It's nearly midnight!"

"Hey, that's okay!" he replied, pulling her to her feet. "Come on, we need to polish our swing a little bit."

"Okay, okay," Pat said laughing. Kevin whirled around, performing exaggerated dance steps over to a nearby CD player, and with a final grandiose gesture, put in the "Memories" disc. Pushing the dining table aside, he struck a dancer's pose and bowed low, requesting, "May I have this dance, Madame?"

Pat loved the way Kevin could talk, grin and make her laugh all at the same time . . . it was an endearing trait. Kevin could always make her laugh—always had—and she was certain it was part of Andrea's attraction to Kevin . . . he was simply *fun*!

"Why, of *course*, Good Sir," Pat replied, curtsying in response.

The opening strains of music echoed in the kitchen, and she did her best to keep up with Kevin. He and Andrea had taken ballroom dance lessons in preparation for the wedding, and she had to admit he had become pretty good with the steps. He was a strong lead, and this certainly helped her stay on the beat. Pat was admittedly not the best dancer, still needing to count in her head the 1-2-3, 1-2-3 rock step—but she did so love dancing with her son.

They continued to practice, playing the song again and again and laughing their way through her mistakes each time.

"Okay, Kev," Pat said, gasping for breath after the fourth time through the song. "That's about all the swing dancing I can do in one night! But thank you for a wonderful dance, Good Sir."

Kevin kissed her on the cheek.

"The pleasure was all mine, Madame!"

"Do you want a snack?" Pat said, pushing the table back into place.

"Sure, what's ya got?"

"I made chocolate no-bakes earlier," she offered, holding out a plate of cookies, knowing what his response would be.

"Great!" Kevin said enthusiastically. "Lots of peanut butter, right?"

"Just the way you like them," Pat smiled as Kevin lifted one off the plate.

"Mmmmm . . . .They're *perfect*," he replied, enjoying his first bite.

"I also have a new box of Cheez-its," she added with a smile. The crackers were his favorite.

"Excellent!" Kevin said opening the box with a grin.

"So, it seems like most of your friends are getting married this summer, huh?" Pat commented, easing herself into a kitchen table chair.

"Yeah, it's funny, and it feels a little bit weird," he replied thoughtfully, helping himself to another cookie. "I guess everyone graduated from college, and now we're all getting married. Can you believe Andrea and I have *eleven* weddings to attend this year?!"

Pat laughed.

"Well, you won't lack for something to do on the weekends, that's for sure!" she reflected, turning back to her cooled mug of tea. "How do you think everyone will do? Any surprises in who is marrying who?"

"Well, yeah. In some ways," Kevin replied. "It *is* kind of weird that 'the other Jeff' is marrying the girl I dated for almost two years in high school. But I think they're good together."

"And I think some people were surprised by Andrea and me," he added. "But that's going to be good, too. You know how you said that researchers tell us that most couples disagree about either money, sex, or in-laws?"

"Yep, those are the big three," Pat confirmed with a nod.

"Well, I don't know that we'll have a lot of disagreements in any of these areas," he said, munching on a cracker. "I might be wrong, but we did go to an engagement seminar weekend, and we found out that we really are on the same page with most things."

"You know what still boggles my mind, Mom?" Kevin said, suddenly turning serious.

"No, what's that?" Pat asked, meeting his gaze to take in every shared thought, emotion, and facial expression.

How I wish I could slow down time and stay in this moment forever!

"How much Andrea loves me," Kevin replied earnestly, seemingly amazed at the thought.

"Well, she *is* a *very* smart woman," Pat said with certainty, emotion choking her voice a bit. "And she's a beautiful girl—she will make a gorgeous bride."

The two sat in silence for a moment as Pat envisioned the couple on their approaching wedding day. Andrea was the same height as Kevin, but with dark hair and brown eyes that contrasted with his dark blonde hair and blue-green eyes . . . yes, they were a handsome couple.

And Andrea *would* be a beautiful bride—Pat had been with Andrea when she chose her dress: it was all lace and beading—very traditional—and she was breathtaking in it. Absolutely perfect . . .

"Well, I better get to bed," Kevin said rising to his feet with a sigh. "I *do* have to be an engineer again tomorrow!"

"Yeah, you're right," Pat replied, reluctant to have the evening end. "It's going to be a busy week; I guess we both better get some sleep."

"Goodnight, Mom," Kevin said, giving her a peck on the cheek. "I love you."

"Goodnight, Honey," she replied, kissing him. "I love you, too."

Sleep did not come easily for Pat that night. She found herself tossing and turning, replaying the nearly twenty-four years of memories with her son in her mind. Kevin: so animated, so unrestrained, so open, so social—he had always been an absolute joy.

Unlike his three older brothers, Kevin had always been a bit of a 'ham,' seizing any opportunity to steal the show like, when he danced on the stage during Christmas programs at church—even when no one else was dancing!

At three, he did a pretty good imitation of 'the Rudy dance' from *The Cosby Show*, and he had loved to play his portable keyboard, donning a hat and sunglasses and performing for the whole family all through his toddler years.

And, Pat recalled with a tear and smile, it had been Kevin who had vowed to marry her when he grew up—he had been four at the time!

As a student, Kevin was bright and always had lots of friends . . . *and* girlfriends. And Pat never ceased to be amazed at how willing he was to talk so openly about his dates, sharing lots of the types of things his brothers would never have even considered telling her. She recalled that on one occasion in high school he came home from an evening out with a girl and seemed genuinely puzzled.

"I thought *everyone* knew how to kiss, Mom!" he had confided to her over a late-night snack. "But apparently *not*. This girl? She *cannot* kiss."

Pat had watched him grow from soccer and Little League to middle school and basketball. In high school, he had discovered cross country and track—and those had been his favorite.

Many of his fellow cross-country runners had made Kevin's house their place to hang out during their high school years. The grocery bills had been a little higher during those years, but the cost was more than worth experiencing the energy those kids had brought into the house.

Pat found that she had really missed all of Kevin's friends being in the house since he'd gone off to college. They were certainly a great group of kids, helping each other grow emotionally, mentally and spiritually.

Not to say that Kevin and his friends hadn't engaged in their share of mischief and pranks over the years, toilet-papering the yards of coaches, teachers, and friends, or on one occasion, even completely filling their cross-country coach's mailbox with M&Ms. Pat knew that she had been lucky with Kevin; his antics had mostly been just goofy, adolescent fun.

Pat reflected on how different Kevin was from the rest of the family. Perhaps it was because he hadn't been shy as a child . . . Or maybe it was because he was more social, outgoing, and happy-go-lucky. Perhaps he was simply more resilient—or maybe because he was younger, Kevin didn't bear evidence of some of the scars that plagued his brothers.

In any case, Pat believed that everyone in the Palmer family sometimes secretly wished they were more like Kevin . . . .she knew *she* did.

Pat tossed and turned a bit more, restlessly turning her thoughts to Kevin's upcoming wedding. For months, she had prayed every night that the day would be perfect for both of them, constantly asking Kevin to think about the little details and worrying about something being forgotten or not going according to plans.

Pat now chided herself, though, as she realized that somewhere along the way she had lost sight of the fact that it was marriage itself that was infinitely more important and valuable than the wedding.

Lord, help me to be a good mother-in-law, Pat breathed a prayer as she finally drifted to sleep. *And give Kevin and Andrea an extraordinary love.*

That was the best kind—of *that* she was certain.

Chapter Twelve
Never Ending Love

Pat's eyelids felt heavy as she lifted them. Chiding herself for staying up too late the night before, she slowly sat up, looking around the room and feeling a little disoriented. Then, a smile spread slowly across her face as she once again remembered where she was and why.

Rays of sunshine poured through the window, casting shadows playfully around the hotel room as clouds passed in front of the sun set in a brilliant blue sky.

It was, she thought to herself with satisfaction, a perfect day for a wedding. Pat smiled again. Today, her baby was walking down the aisle. Today was Kevin's wedding day!

The months leading up to this moment seemed a blur, looking back. And perhaps the thrill of being Mother-of-the-Groom would never be the same as if she'd been on the roller coaster of emotions that accompanies being Mother-of-the-Bride . . . But Pat knew instinctively that today was special. Very special. And the butterflies in her stomach in anticipation of the day ahead reminded her of another special summer day years before.

A smile spread across her face as flash-frame moments from a day in her own past flashed across her mind's eye: smiles, tears, butterflies and the magical surety of a golden future just beyond the horizon . . .

My wedding day was just incredible! Dear God, please let this day be just as special for my Kevin . . .

She climbed from the bed, her excitement of the day ahead growing. The day and night before had been a whirlwind: the drive to southwest Michigan, followed by the wedding rehearsal. Afterwards, a rehearsal dinner had taken place at a small Italian restaurant in the picturesque little community of Zeeland. Pat had smiled contentedly as attendees took turns telling stories about the happy couple.

She had relished looking around the room, seeing so many dear and familiar faces sharing in her happiness. Suezell and her husband sat chatting with other family members, along with members of Andrea's family. Matt and Heidi bantered back and forth with Jeff and his friends, Sarah and Andrea, who had come along, jokingly referring to themselves as his 'dates.' Kevin was grinning ear-to-ear, and Pat couldn't help but notice the affectionate way Andrea nestled under his arm.

Everyone was in good spirits when they arrived back to the hotel, sitting in the hotel hallway outside of their rooms, laughing and talking and telling stories. Kevin was spending the evening with Andrea, and Pat had enlisted Sarah and Andrea to help 'toilet-paper' and ransack Kevin's hotel room for the night. The hour was late when they had all finally settled in for the evening.

"Mom?" a whisper had said, "You still awake?"

Pat had groggily opened the hotel room door hours later to find Kevin outside.

His easy-going grin was unmistakably Jim's.

"Nice touches to my room," he laughed. "I guess it's payback for what I did to Matt the night before his wedding."

"I don't know what you're talking about," Pat replied with an affectionate smile. "I have witnesses that can account for my whereabouts the entire evening."

Kevin chuckled before suddenly turning serious.

"Um, Mom? Can I ask you something?"

"Of course you can!" Pat had tightened her robe around her

and stepped out into the hallway. "What is it?"

"I guess I just . . . well, tomorrow's a big day—probably the biggest day of my life . . . "

Pat smiled again. She knew that feeling: the feeling that tomorrow was going to be important, exciting, and thrilling! And nothing else mattered in the world except that tomorrow would soon be here . . .

Kevin continued. "I guess I just wanted to say 'thanks'. Thanks for showing me how to be the kind of person that will love and take care of Andrea for the rest of my life."

Tears had filled Pat's eyes at his simple and heartfelt words. With a kiss on the cheek and a hug, Kevin had bid her goodnight and said "See you in the morning, Mom! It's gonna be a great day!"

Pat had gone back into her hotel room, his words echoing in her ears and knowing exactly how he was feeling that night. As she crawled back into bed and closed her eyes, the past suddenly called to her once again . . .

It was the happiest day of my entire life, a day I'd only dreamed of. Looking back, I often relive the moments over and over again: the look in Jim's eyes while I was walking toward him, the flutter of my own heart as he placed a band of gold on my finger, the thrill of hearing the words "I now pronounce you man and wife . . . "

"See you in the morning, Mom!" Pat called from her bedroom, certain she wouldn't be able to sleep. The list of things she still needed to do before tomorrow should've been racing through her head, but it didn't seem to matter. She was tired and wanted to get a good night's sleep before the big day tomorrow. She had stayed visiting with her family till late before excusing herself for the night, half-wondering if her mother would be close behind to finally have "the talk" in preparation for her wedding night . . . but in reality, the only thing her mother had ever indicated to her about sex was the fact that she never wore panties to bed at night!

Perhaps that was part of the anticipation she felt tonight; but even more so was the surge of excitement to begin a new life tomorrow! Never in her life had Pat imagined that she could be this happy and in-love! It somehow didn't matter that the list of things to do before tomorrow afternoon was long. It somehow didn't matter that her dress was just so-so in her mind. It didn't even matter that the forecast was calling for rain.

All Pat knew was that tomorrow she would become Mrs. Jim Palmer, and she had never been so certain of anything in her entire life . . . It was a blissful thought to fall asleep with . . .

Hours later, Pat's eyelids felt heavy as she lifted them. Downstairs, she could hear her mother already bustling around, making coffee and starting breakfast. She slowly sat up, looking around the room and feeling a little disoriented. Then, a smile spread across her face as she once again remembered where she was and why . . . Today, she was marrying the love of her life.

Pat knew she should get up and begin preparations for the day, but she couldn't resist a few minutes to herself before the whirlwind began. She had always considered herself practical, but today . . . today was special! And somehow her pragmatic side had vanished. There was so much to be done: hair appointments for her, Mom, and Suezell; she really should call the flower shop to make sure everything would be delivered to the church on time, and her nails needed a light coat of clear polish . . . But somehow, in that moment, practicality and thoughtful planning to stay on schedule before a two o'clock wedding seemed ridiculous and unimportant. All Pat wanted to do was linger under her quilt, suddenly aware that today was a bridge between two lifetimes: a childhood that she was letting go of and a future of happiness that she was embracing.

She laid back, stretching her frame across the bed, reflecting for a moment as the strangeness of it all sank in.

Pat had heard of pre-wedding jitters. She'd heard whispered confessions of brides having second thoughts on the day they awoke and realized they were about to commit to one man, one home, one family for the rest of their lives. Pat smiled contentedly with the warm glow of someone who just *knew* she'd made the right choice. She just *knew*! Jim was the love of her life, the one and only man she wanted to marry, live with, share a bed, home, children—share a life! It was Jim! He was *the one* . . .

Her thoughts suddenly shifted for a moment as she realized just how unusual her bliss was! How strange, wonderful and exciting that she of all the people in the world had been given a storybook romance . . . her very own *fairytale*!

The day ahead almost seemed too good to be true—too magical to be my reality! I was, after all, just a girl from a small town in a small state in a small world . . . How in the world did I get to be so, so lucky?!

As if on cue, there was a knock at the bedroom door.

"Pat?" her sister's voice whispered, "Are you awake yet?"

"Come on in," Pat called softly.

The door opened, and Suezell glided across the room, dramatically practicing her bridesmaid walk as she hummed the Bridal March. Pat laughed out loud at the sight.

Suezell slid under the covers next to her sister and whispered, "Well, today is *the day*!"

"I know!" Pat whispered back, suddenly realizing that their childhoods were officially ending that morning. It was a bittersweet moment, knowing that whispered conversations, late night giggling, and sisterly chats under the covers would be no more . . .

"What are you thinking about right now?" Suezell asked, her eyes growing misty at the thought of the coming day.

Pat rolled over, propping her head up with one arm. "I was thinking about how my life feels like a fairytale—but then who would've thought that someone ordinary like me would ever have a fairytale?"

A smile spread across Suezell's face, and a knowing look suddenly lit her eyes.

"But Pat, that's what makes you and Jim so special! I think that every once in a while, in an ordinary life, love gives you a fairytale. This is yours! And you both deserve all the happiness in the world . . ."

The tears came then, for both of the sisters. They embraced, and when Pat pulled away she smiled and gently wiped a tear from Suezell's face. They shared another hug, lingering in a final childhood embrace before Pat's practical side once again took over.

"Okay, we'd better get up and get moving," Pat crawled from her bed and struck a pose in front of her mirror. "Today is the day the fairytale comes true!"

The smell of early summer earth and imminent rain hung in the air. The church was stark and white against an overcast sky and seemed to be framed by the surrounding fields of early growth from the farms nearby. I stepped from the car still marveling at how calm I was, and walked up the church sidewalk.

Funny that I should remember the walk so vividly. It was one of those moments that I knew without a shadow of a doubt would echo in my mind for the rest of my life. I found myself staring at the steeple, noticing that it seemed to be pointing straight to God. I knew He was present that day, as sure as I knew that my dress was snowy white and that Jim and our friends and family were waiting inside.

Please God, I silently prayed, Give us a happy life together!

At that moment, a ray of sunshine split through the gray clouds. It was as if God Himself was smiling down on me, urging me to understand and cherish the simple beauty of the moment. I smiled back toward the heavens as my father opened the church doors . . .

"Wait just one minute, Pat," Pat's mother said, nervously fussing with her train for the tenth time in the past few moments. Pat exchanged a knowing smile with her father, and calmly replied:

"It's okay, Mom. The train is fine. It's time to let go now."

Standing in the foyer of the church, Pat could already hear the music playing, and the gentle anticipatory murmur of friends and family waiting inside the auditorium. Ahead of her, waiting in line to enter the sanctuary, stood Debbie and Suezell and Jim's sister-in-law, Darlene, all of them looking beautiful in bright azalea pink and white chiffon gowns, white and lacy wide-brimmed straw hats on their heads. They carried baskets of mixed flowers—roses, baby carnations, and tulips . . . They were beautiful—in fact, in that moment, everything seemed beautiful and soft and right.

Pat caught her own reflection in a nearby window and smiled in satisfaction. Sheer white fabric fell gracefully from an empire waist, revealing white satin beneath and ribbons running from the shoulder to the floor. A modest train cascaded from her waist, lined with lace and a satin ribbon. Her veil was simple, flowing over hair piled on top of her head, and she carried a bouquet of pink roses, carnations and baby's breath.

Pat again was amazed, though, at how little she really cared about her appearance at the moment. Nothing really mattered except the next few moments of her life. Suezell turned her head just in time to give a subtle wink and a grin as the bridesmaids began their walk toward the altar. Seconds later, her father squeezed her hand, his eyes staring forward and misting slightly.

Every once in a while, in an ordinary life, love gives you a fairytale . . .

Pat smiled calmly as the opening strains of the Bridal Chorus echoed in her ears. She stepped in the sanctuary, vaguely aware of friends and family rising to their feet smiling. Only one thing held her full attention: Jim was standing at the front near the minister, his eyes twinkling and grin beaming as though life's greatest prize was walking toward him. Pat's eyes were sparkling as she reached the altar and took Jim's hands in hers.

Suezell was quietly weeping what Pat knew were tears of both joy and sadness—and Pat noticed Jim's brother and best man, Ted, hand her a handkerchief. Pat was also aware of her father's tear-stained face, delighted for her and yet certainly feeling the ache of Tom's absence on such a special day.

Pat knew that a hundred years from now she'd never be able to put into words the emotion of that moment in time. Jim's hands were warm in hers as the ceremony began. His eyes were soft and tender and sparkling, and every now and then, Pat would find the breath catch in her throat at the sheer bliss of what was taking place.

I am becoming Mrs. Jim Palmer! She repeated the name over and over again in her head, deliriously happy with the sound. *God, thank you for sending me such a wonderful man! Thank you, thank you, thank you!*

Jim's voice broke into her thoughts.

"I take you, Pat, to be my wife, my lifetime companion and the mother of my children," he said, his eyes misting over. "I have longed for and sought after one with whom I could share my life."

" In you," he continued. "I have found the one whom I can share my joys, sorrows; hopes and plans; strengths and weaknesses. I accept you as you are and because of my love for you, I also accept and love your family as our family."

Pat smiled delightedly as his face broke into a grin—that same grin that had caught her stare the first moment she had seen him.

"God has given us His greatest gift: love, and through Him, I am able to both receive and give this gift," he said, his voice clear and strong. "So, today, I make you this promise: You will have my full and constant love from this day forward until death us do part."

In that moment, my heart nearly burst with love. The world was suspended in time: a dreamy hazy sort of reality tinting the room with golden warmth, and a peace settling around the moment as I pledged to love Jim Palmer for all of eternity . . .

"I take you, Jim, to be my husband, my lifetime companion, and the father of my children. My search has ended. I, too, have longed for the one with whom I could share my life. In you, I have found one with whom I can share all my joys, sorrows, goals and ambitions and strengths and weaknesses. I accept you as you are, and because of my love for you, I also accept and love your family as our family."

Pat's voice quivered ever so slightly as she continued.

"I thank God for giving me you to love and be loved by; and so today, I make you this promise: You will have my full and constant love from this day forward until death us do part."

The rest of the ceremony was a blur: Jim and Pat lit a unity candle, and Pat heard a voice reading from I Corinthians' 13th chapter. As if in a dream, she watched Jim slip a gold band onto her left hand with a meaningful squeeze as he whispered, "Never ending love, Angel!"

Chapter Thirteen
State of Bliss

"Honeymoon."

I didn't know exactly where the expression had come from—I had heard that it had something to do with an ancient tradition dating back to the Greeks or Romans—or someone like that . . . In reality, I could only think of one word to accurately describe my honeymoon: "bliss."

It felt as though we were on an island, magically protected from the dangers and worries of the day-to-day world, as though we were the first couple who ever basked in true love in our own Garden of Eden . . .

Our wedding reception was brief—wedding cake, punch and well-wishes from family and friends. Soon, we bid our guests goodbye and headed north to Clare, just thirty-five miles away. I remember feeling like a princess in my lavender and pink flower-print dress with its white peter pan collar.

Our car was, of course, decorated with 'just married' signs, and other cars on the highway honked their horns and cheered as I waved my bridal bouquet in response. It was as if the entire universe was created just for our pleasure: a whole wonderful world of green fields, blue skies and people celebrating—just because of our love!

We spent our first night at the historic, elegant Doherty Hotel in Clare. My mom had given me a beautiful sheer white lace negligee set. It was feminine, soft, and sweet, and when I emerged from the bathroom wearing it, Jim just beamed at me, exclaiming softly, "Oh, Angel, you look so beautiful!"

I was Mrs. Jim Palmer**,** and I simply couldn't stop smiling. The *way he looked at me that night was like being wrapped in a blanket of unconditional love and adoration.*

We were each other's firsts, and our lovemaking was incredible, a true expression of love. There was complete acceptance and an intense desire to pleasure one another. We made love again and again that night, savoring each time and delighting in the thrill of being husband and wife. It was the greatest pleasure I had ever known—for so, so many reasons . . .

We began a tradition that night that continued for the years to come: each time we made love, after experiencing the ultimate, exhilarating pleasure, I would breathlessly tell Jim, "Thank you!" And, from that day forward, there were always thank-yous in our bed . . .

Still, we always cherished that first night together. We found ourselves laughing and smiling, cuddling and promising we would sleep— only to find ourselves entwined once more.

The next day, we "slept late" of course, and slowly made our way north to Mackinaw City. We didn't really have an agenda and took our time stopping whenever we wanted. The weather was cool for June, but we hardly noticed. The radio kept playing Donna Fargo's popular song, "I'm The Happiest Girl In The Whole U.S.A."

It was my theme song for that week, perfectly describing how I felt: the whole experience was surreal, and I kept wanting to pinch myself as a kind of reality check—but it was all true! This was me! I was really married to Jim Palmer at last! I was loved by a fantastic, 'most wonderful man God ever made' guy!

I remember smiling, leaning on his shoulder while he drove, and singing along with the radio. Bliss—what a state in which to live . . .

The weather was overcast and cool as the newlyweds arrived in Mackinaw City, Michigan—but to the new Mrs. Palmer, the sun was shining in a vibrant blue sky dotted with seagulls and perfect wispy white clouds. The Mackinaw Bridge, a recognizable Michigan landmark connecting the state's two peninsulas, stood tall and strong and beautiful against the choppy waters of the

Straits of Mackinaw where Lakes Michigan and Huron collided and freighter ships passed ancient lighthouses still guiding sailors through the often-stormy passageway.

It was nearly noon when Pat and Jim parked their car, ready to browse the tourist shops on the town's main street and find a place to eat lunch. Mackinaw City had become increasingly geared toward tourism over the years, and the couple passed shop windows displaying an assortment of tourist items: t-shirts, souvenir glasses, paperweights, banners, and the world-famous Mackinaw fudge.

The displays were tempting, but the ever-practical couple kept their budget in mind, recording every cent they spent on the honeymoon thus far. With that in mind, they had so far avoided the lure of souvenirs, choosing instead to stroll past the shops hand-in-hand, filled with the excitement and anticipation of spending a lifetime together.

They decided to have lunch at The Lighthouse, a casual-dining bistro near the shoreline.

"I think I'll have a hot roast beef sandwich," Jim told the waitress as she asked for their orders.

Pat smiled in amusement, ordering a tuna salad sandwich for herself and iced teas for both of them.

"What's so funny, Angel?" Jim asked, taking her hand and squeezing it affectionately as the waitress hurried off.

"You *always* order a hot roast beef sandwich," Pat teased, squeezing his hand back.

"Well, you know, in my family, we never ate out unless it was absolutely impossible to be home at mealtime," Jim laughed. "My parents always ordered hot roast beef sandwiches in restaurants—I didn't know you could order anything else!"

The two o'clock ferry left the Arnold Line dock with Pat and Jim aboard, joining fifty other travelers enroute to Michigan's historic Mackinac Island. The pair selected seats on the lower deck in an effort to avoid the chilly breeze coming off of Lake Huron.

The sky had cleared a bit, and through the smudged windows of the boat's seating section, the island looked crisp and green against the sky in the distance. Jim and Pat snuggled together against the damp chill in the air, exchanging glances and smiles like two giddy teenagers, chattering excitedly about their plans to visit the Island and spend a night at the world-famous Grand Hotel.

"Oh, let's go up to the top deck and see the view," Pat suddenly blurted out impulsively. "I don't care if it's cold!"

The two climbed to the top deck, laughing a bit as they fought to keep their balance on the moving ferry boat. The icy wind coming off of Lake Huron in the boat's wake took their breath away, but then, so did the view.

Mackinac Island looked beautiful, shimmering on the distant horizon ahead of them like the setting for a fairytale. In the early years of Michigan's history, the island had been a stopping point for a lucrative fur trade involving the French, English and Native Americans living in the territory. Later, the island served as a vantage point during the Revolutionary War and the War of 1812 in the battle to control Great Lakes travel and shipping routes. Then came an era of fishing in the 1830's, drawing Irish immigrants away from the potato famine-ridden lands back home to the shores of Michigan's own similar island paradise.

It was as if time itself froze during this period. Now home to the direct descendants of the original French-Native and Irish families, things hadn't changed much, and Mackinac Island prided itself on taking visitors back in time to an era of horse-drawn carriages, lush natural settings, and elegant historic hotels.

The island came into clearer focus as the boat drew closer, and Pat snuggled against Jim.

"I love you, Jim Palmer," she whispered contentedly.

He grinned at her.

"I love you more."

"Impossible," she countered, shaking her head.

"*Not* impossible," Jim responded, kissing her cheek.

"A tie?" she asked, squeezing his hand.

"A tie," he agreed with a nod.

Twenty minutes later, the ferry docked on the island, and the couple was greeted by the cries of seagulls and by a mixture of fragrant lilacs, sweet-smelling chocolate fudge, and horses. The Island was indeed a portal through time with its historic Victorian homes, quaint shops and hotels graced with gingerbread trim, striped awnings, and white picket fences.

Pat sighed blissfully, taking in the sight. Tulips, geraniums, and lilac bushes were neatly tended in every yard and store front window box, and the peaceful, constant clip-clop of horses was both nostalgic and soothing. Declining offers from horse drawn taxicab drivers, the couple opted to make the short walk to the hotel.

Moving further away from Main Street, the air grew quieter as they turned onto a wide, tree-lined avenue that sloped up to a sprawling, elegant building, Michigan's very own Grand Hotel.

The elegant building and grounds had been a famous Michigan landmark since its opening in 1887, drawing the upper class of tourists seeking to escape the summer heat and hay fever in places like Chicago, Montreal and Detroit. Maintaining popularity past the turn of the century, audiences all over the country were introduced to the lavish hotel as the setting for Hollywood starlet Esther Williams' movie, *This Time for Keeps*. Later on, the hotel would be permanently etched into the minds of star-crossed lovers as the site for the tragic romance, *Somewhere in Time*.

But today! Today, the Grand Hotel was the site for a simple couple from Mid-Michigan, desperately in love and happily beginning a new life together. Pat kissed Jim's cheek as they began the stroll up the street to the hotel. It was going to be a perfect evening!

The Grand Hotel was busy with guests arriving by carriage, bellhops whisking bags into the foyer, and patrons and visitors taking pictures or sipping drinks on the vast front porch. Grand Hotel sported the longest front porch in the world, stretching the entire length of the nearly four hundred guest room building, curving away from the bustling entryway to romantic and breathtaking views of Lake Huron and the Straits of Mackinaw just over the treeline.

Jim squeezed Pat's hand. It really was the perfect romantic setting. The inviting porch was filled with white wicker furniture with plush green and white striped cushions, and huge pots of red geraniums seemingly invited them to be a part of the fairytale scene around them.

Both Pat and Jim had visited Mackinac Island separately before on school fieldtrips and family outings, but today! Today, was the first time either had entered the grand foyer of the landmark Hotel. They stepped inside to find the interior vibrant with color, typical of the era in which the hotel was built. The carpet was emerald green, sprinkled with coral pink geraniums; red and green velvet cushions donned ornately-carved chairs and Victorian benches scattered around the spacious lobby. Ornate vases of fresh flowers topped case pieces throughout the room, and chandeliers reflected the glistening brilliance of the colors coming from everywhere.

It was mid-afternoon, and the hotel staff was busily preparing for formal tea with beautiful delicate treats displayed on silver trays next to dainty floral tea cups in Victorian blues, greens, yellows, pinks, and reds. Soft music drifted in and out above the lobby din, and Pat noticed a harpist positioned in the far corner, drawing her fingers over the strings with poise and grace. There was so much to take in that the couple just stood agape for a moment, gazing at the magnificence of it all. It was even beyond their expectations.

The couple approached the front desk and waited a moment for the clerk to finish up with another guest. After a moment, he smiled at them expectantly.

"Name?" he asked.

"Mr. and Mrs. Jim Palmer," Jim replied with a grin.

The clerk smiled and replied, "Ah, yes, Mr. Palmer, we have your reservation right here. This is your honeymoon, correct?"

Pat squeezed Jim's arm and he smiled.

"That's right," Jim beamed. "This is my beautiful wife, Pat."

"Well, it's nice to meet you, Pat!" the clerk replied cordially. "I think you two will like your room. Since it's early in the season and a weekday, we were able to place you in one of our luxury suites."

"Why, thank you!" Pat exclaimed in delight.

Jim grinned.

"That's really nice of you!"

"The pleasure is all ours," the staffer insisted with a wink. "We take special care of honeymooners here at the Grand."

"Well, your luggage has been delivered to your room," the clerk continued, handing Jim a key. "All you have left to do is enjoy your stay!"

The pair climbed the ornate staircase nearby to the third floor and followed the corridor to the right until they found their bags neatly piled next to the door of room 321.

Jim turned the key, and the door opened. He scooped Pat up into his arms.

"Angel, this is it," he said kissing her neck tenderly as he carried her over the threshold.

Still nestled in Jim's arms, Pat took in the room around her. The room was a palette of pinks, mauves and reds. The wallpaper was a lattice pattern in yellow and white. The bath door was open, revealing it to be vibrant Victorian pink, complete with pink geranium soaps, plush white towels and bath robes.

French doors opened out onto a balcony with a beautiful view of the landmark Round Island Lighthouse, the Grand Hotel lawn and gardens sweeping away from the building toward the shoreline, and even the Mackinaw Bridge on the horizon. It was all simply breathtaking; a dream come true . . .

With a contented sigh, her lips met Jim's.

"Thank you, thank you, thank you!" she murmured, trailing kisses down his neck.

He chuckled.

"Hey, there," he whispered with a shiver of pleasure at her touch. "Wait for me with those 'thank yous'! I'm sure this place has a bed somewhere."

Pat blushed as Jim set her down.

A queen-sized bed was enveloped in a canopy of white tulle, and the satin bedspread was sprinkled with bouquets of pink and yellow.

"Well, it's pretty nice!" Jim observed with a teasing grin. "Good thing I'm okay with pink, huh?"

"That's for sure," Pat nodded, still a bit breathless in anticipation. She circled her arms around him and leaned her head on his chest. "And you probably should get used to it—you do realize that's my favorite color, right?"

"Oh! That explains it!" Jim exclaimed as he tenderly trailed his fingers down her cheek. "So *that's* why I was wearing a pink shirt at the wedding—come to think of it, the bridesmaids were in pink, too, weren't they?"

"Very funny," Pat retorted with a smirk, standing on tiptoe to kiss the tip of his nose.

"Well, we do have two hours before dinner is served, Madame," Jim said, staring into her eyes and slipping into his best British accent. "Whatever shall we do in the meantime? I haven't the faintest idea . . . "

She smiled sheepishly as he lifted her gently onto the bed.

"I love you, Angel," he said, staring deeply into her eyes before pulling her into another kiss.

She melted at his touch.

"I love you, too," she whispered breathlessly before losing herself in passion once more.

I really am the luckiest girl in the whole U.S.A . . .

Later the couple found themselves ready to dress for dinner. Jim had brought along his navy blue wedding suit, with a crisp, white shirt and a blue tie.

Pat smiled at her husband; he was brilliantly handsome, as always.

Pat had selected for herself a white lace dress with short sleeves and a modest v-neck. The skirt was short and full, perfect for the evening with her pearl earrings, which were her 21st birthday present from Jim.

Jim and Pat walked past the registration desk, hand in hand, noticing the gray-haired gentleman who had checked them in. He smiled at them knowingly and asked, "And how is your room, Mr. and Mrs. Palmer?"

They both smiled shyly, assuring him it was perfect. He smiled in satisfaction.

"It's like I told you—we take good care of honeymooners here at the Grand."

Waiters in tuxedos greeted them at the hotel dining room entrance and led them to a candlelit table for two. The china was simple and elegant on the white linen tablecloths. Each table was adorned with a small bouquet of fresh deep purple lilacs from the Island's world-famous Lilac Festival, along with pale yellow tulips. Jim smiled as he caught Pat's eyes light up as she took in their surroundings.

The waiter promptly arrived at their table with large, freshly-printed menus featuring choices for each of the five-course dinners.

"Uh-oh, Honey," Pat teased, patting Jim's arm. "I don't see hot roast beef on the menu. Whatever are you going to order?"

Jim grinned good-naturedly.

"Yeah, I guess this is a little out of my league, huh?" he

responded with a laugh.

"Well, I'm going to have the shrimp cocktail for my appetizer," Pat announced after a moment. "What looks good to you?"

Jim selected a puff pastry filled with crab salad and cream cheese. It arrived beautifully garnished with a fresh miniature orchid on top. The choices were delicious, and the two anticipated the soup that would soon be served, a more-familiar potato leek broth appealed to what Jim jokingly dubbed their 'down-home taste buds.' The salads that followed were an artistic display of greens, candied walnuts, Michigan dried cherries, and fresh strawberries.

Both Jim and Pat were feeling satisfied even before their main entrees were served, but it didn't stop them from heartily enjoying them. Jim chose the tenderloin, even after Pat teased him about it really just being a fancier version of a roast beef sandwich, and Pat chose the Great Lakes' specialty whitefish.

For dessert, Pat decided on the hotel's signature pecan ice cream ball smothered in hot fudge sauce. Jim was equally pleased with his all-American favorite warm apple and caramel pie with vanilla bean ice cream.

"Good thing we got some good exercise in before dinner," Jim said, winking at his new bride as he sipped some after-dinner coffee. "That was something else, wasn't it?"

"It was unbelievable," Pat agreed, squeezing his hand under the table. "Now, Honey, just because I'm a home-ec teacher, I hope you don't expect this type of meal every night."

"Oh, but I most certainly do!" Jim teased her, placing a kiss on her cheek.

Following dinner, the couple were drawn to the live band playing standard ballads in the terrace room and danced to some of the slower melodies. Neither of them were exceptional dancers, but they enjoyed the opportunity to be in each other's arms, whispering into the other's ear as they held each other.

The moon was full and bright, and the pair couldn't resist the urge to be a part of the summer evening, walking the length of the Grand porch before they returned to their room. It was cool with the lake breeze drifting in off of the shimmering water.

Pat shivered, and Jim gallantly draped his suit jacket over her shoulders. She sighed contentedly, enjoying every moment of a fantasy come true: moonlight, music, romance, flowers, and the love of her life . . .

Jim pulled her into his embrace, warming her body against his as her heart began racing.

So, this is what it's like to be blissfully, happily married . . .

Later that evening, Pat dressed in a new soft pink negligee: short, flirty, and feminine. Jim gave a low whistle in approval as she stepped from the bathroom.

Boy, for a guy who, a few months ago, thought a "barrette" was a small pub, Pat thought with amusement. *He is certainly getting an education on girly-girls!*

Jim was, on the other hand, sticking to the basics: white J.C. Penney underwear. Observing his tan hairy chest and trim body, Pat decided that 'the basics' were just fine with her.

She crossed the room and cuddled up next to her husband, kissing his lips and stroking his face tenderly.

"I love you," she said, staring up into his eyes. "You know that, right?"

He smiled at her.

"I do."

The couple basked in their love once more.

Morning came, and the Palmers stayed as long as possible in the pink fantasy room with the pillowy bed, barely making the noon check-out time.

The sun was shining and bright as the ferry boat made their Mackinac Island paradise smaller and smaller on the horizon. Today, they planned to cross the Mackinac Bridge and travel along Lake

Michigan, heading west enjoying the blue skies and breathtaking views of sandstone bluffs and sparkling water along the way. Mid-afternoon, they stopped to walk the beach, dip their toes in the icy waters, and take silly pictures of one another laughing and making faces. That night, their hotel room in a small town in Michigan's Upper Peninsula was typical—except for the exceptional love and passion they brought with them.

By the next day, Pat had developed a headcold and spent much of their travel time nodding off on Jim's shoulder. He smiled, reassuring her several times that it was fine; that he was content just to be with his new wife. She kissed him drowsily, grateful again for the wonderful man she married.

Pat roused sufficiently to take the short hike back to the Michigan landmark, Taquammon Falls, as the couple made their way back toward the Straits of Mackinaw. The beauty of thundering copper-colored water, framed in a setting of poplar and evergreen was breathtaking.

Pat smiled up at her husband as they watched the water cascade to swirling pools fifty feet below.

They were both thinking the same thought: *It's time.*

It's time to go home, explore our wedding gifts, and begin our lives as husband and wife . . .

CHAPTER FOURTEEN
Extraordinary Love

Looking back now, I realize that I had no idea just how lucky I was. But then, I was in what my mother would've called 'a blissful bubble.' Maybe most brides feel that way, maybe not. But for me, there was absolutely no way of knowing how phenomenal married life could be. I have never witnessed anything before or since that compares to our lives together. It was truly extraordinary.

I was in a state of happiness with an incredible man who worshiped the ground I walked on. He adored me, although I still am not sure why—but he really and truly did.

Looking back now, I know how rare was our love, but it probably didn't completely take form in my mind until years into the marriage. At that moment, I was just blissfully happy and in love . . . and I was the new Mrs. Jim Palmer . . .

Mr. and Mrs. Jim Palmer returned from their honeymoon to begin their lives together in a 12x50 foot mobile home in Millington, Michigan. Pat had to admit that it was a little bit like playing house, just as she had done a thousand times with Suezell as a child. She knew that their little 'lovenest' felt absolutely perfect for the family living/life skills teacher-bride and her handyman/engineer/teacher husband who was working as a painter at the school during the summer to earn extra money.

That summer, Pat spent her days unpacking wedding gifts and writing thank-you notes, all the while accessorizing their home with throw pillows, candles, and dishes received from friends and relatives. Each night, she had dinner prepared for her husband and almost every night they ate by candlelight—even if the entire dinner consisted of a mere tuna noodle casserole.

Pat stubbornly insisted that it was more romantic that way, and Jim simply smiled, delighting in her feminine romantic touches on their world. He looked forward to spending every evening with her, cuddling, talking about everything from the future to their fall teaching schedules—even the need to purchase a washer and dryer—all things that all new couples discuss. But mostly, Mr. and Mrs. Palmer held each other, smiled at the blissfulness of marriage, and expressed their love every night as they were entwined together.

Autumn arrived, and classes began for both of them. Pat relished buying new clothes for her new husband and, of course, finding new outfits for herself to begin a new school year.

As the year began, she had an hour-drive to her school near Port Huron, but she would be teaching in a junior and senior high combination schedule so she started her day at ten a.m. and was finished at three p.m. It was a wonderful schedule for her, and it eased the crowded situation in the 1972 school system.

Pat was teaching interior design, child development, foods and nutrition, and clothing and textiles—a lot to prep for each day—but she had grown used to this schedule since student teaching and didn't mind it. In fact, truth be told, she liked the variety.

Jim had fewer preparations each day, teaching Drafting I and II, along with one section of Metal Shop. He did, however, have a lot of homework assignments to grade. Each night, he brought home stacks of large 10x14 sheets of green drawing papers to grade, always careful to give thorough feedback, circling areas where students' corners were not perfectly aligned, noting the correct architectural lettering form, and checking the correctness of scale used in the drawings. Still, their honeymoon continued, and all of the couple's prep work and paper-grading were mere distractions from their need to hold one another, spending hours kissing and making love. They were completely, madly in love.

I found marriage exactly what I dreamed it would be—only so, so much more. Every day with Jim, I was at once both completely bathrobe-and-slippers comfortable to be myself and simultaneously transported to some unknown galaxy where fairytales came true. Prince Charming was as real as a tulip garden in springtime, and his love blanketed me like one of those Michigan snowfalls that leaves everything soft and glistening and radiant.

I had gone from living my life in black and white to experiencing a life in full, blossoming color. As if I had been a mere silhouette transformed into a lovely portrait, everything was colored by Jim's love. From the simplest, mundane tasks like laundry, dishes, and vacuuming to breathtaking hugs and whispered messages of love, everything in my life was vibrant and forever transformed. I was Mrs. Jim Palmer!

I continued singing my "Someone" song.

It seemed we both had moved from the anonymity of being middle children with average IQs, average looks, and personalities that did not distinguish themselves from the crowd. Now, we belonged to one another, the object of each other's passion.

Suddenly, we were unique miracles of God, created solely for one another. No longer shy, somewhat-awkward individuals, we were a couple, and both of us projected a new demeanor of confidence. Happiness radiated in our smiles, our laughter, and our enthusiasm for life. It was no less a dramatic transformation than Clark Kent entering a phone booth only to emerge as Superman. We were living, breathing proof of the transformational power of extraordinary love . . .

Pat knew that in the early years of marriage, many couples let the flame of romance grow dim in the face of crying babies, loads of laundry, bill-paying, and other tedious tasks that can so easily define a couple's new existence. She knew with complete and utter certainty, however, that this would not be the case with Jim and her. Of course, they had not been typical teenagers or young adults, though, so why would have they been a typical married couple? They were certainly destined to find extraordinary love!

And *extraordinary* certainly defined their relationship—even more during marriage than in their courtship days. It was remarkable and as rare a gift as found on Earth—a slice of Heaven on Earth, in fact. Oh, Pat knew that some would consider that description corny, but that didn't bother her—it was simply the truth.

Six months into their life together as husband and wife, Pat bounded out of the doctor's office, reuniting with Jim in the waiting room and grinning from ear to ear.

"Well, what did the doctor say?" he asked anxiously. "Are you okay?"

"We are going to have a baby, Honey!" she exclaimed, unable to contain her excitement as she threw her arms around him.

Jim beamed at his wife, hugging her tightly.

"Angel, I love you," he whispered into her hair. "And we're going to have a baby." Jim repeated the words, suddenly solemn as if the enormous responsibility of parenthood was slowly sinking in.

Hand in hand, the pair left the doctor's office. A light snow was falling, and the world was still sparkling from an ice storm the day before. Jim reached out to steady Pat as she wobbled on a patch of ice.

"Are you all right?" he said anxiously. "You almost slipped!"

"Oh, I'm fine, Honey," Pat said, affectionately rubbing his shoulder in reassurance, loving his concern. She wondered if Jim was going to be overly-protective with his pregnant wife, but she didn't care if he was. They were having a baby, and they were both ecstatic. Nothing else mattered in the world.

They reached the car, and Jim reached to open the door for her, but Pat took his hand and pulled him toward her.

"I love you, Honey," she said, gazing into his eyes with a loving smile and circling her arms around his waist.

He grinned and pulled her close to him as she leaned her head on his chest.

"I love you more," he whispered tenderly.

"Impossible!" she countered, shaking her head.

"*Not* impossible!" Jim responded, kissing her cheek.

"A tie?" she asked, squeezing his hand.

"A tie." he agreed with a nod, pulling her lips into a passionate kiss.

Nearly eight months later, little Jeff arrived on August 23, 1973, 9 lbs. and 7 oz. with a little reddish hair and already looking just like his Daddy. The tiny infant was accepted as a gift from God and enfolded into their circle of love.

In the months that followed, their world certainly changed—as all lives change with parenthood—but it did not define them. At their very core, Jim and Pat remained deeply in love and totally committed to each other.

Pat would later recall that it was the most unique aspect of Jim's personality. As her friend and mentor, Carolyn, would later say, "Identity determines our actions. Who we *think* we are in any situation or relationship is how we will act."

For Jim, his family was his first love. As the years passed, Jim *always* defined himself as, first of all, Pat's husband, and secondly, as a father. He was an educator, provider, son, brother, friend, colleague *after* he was a husband and father, respectively. His 'Angel' received top priority with his time, affection, protection, and adoration.

Pat knew that for some, it might have seemed smothering, but for her, it was being completely, absolutely loved. She believed that everyone on the face of the earth needed to be the most important person in the world to one other person. She and Jim were always that for one another.

Parenthood was such a joy. In later years, Pat would smile as she thought about how little one recalls of the pain of labor, the sleepless nights, or the struggle with toddlers—all of those memories were overshadowed by the joy of being a couple with a family.

She basked in cherishing every day of family life, appreciating the moments in each phase of their unfolding life together.

Pat Oswald Palmer knew there was a treasure in each day, and that it was simply a person's choice to either hold onto the beauty or let it slip through our fingers as we journey through life. Friends sometimes teased her about her idealistic outlook on life—she was part dreamer, part optimist, and something of a philosophical reflector—but Pat decided she was fine with that!

The treasure chest of memories from our family years is deep and wide and precious. My teen years weren't the best years of my life, as many often say. Rather, the best years of my life were with Jim walking beside me on life's journey, experiencing joy and sorrow, the blissful and the mundane, and simply being a family together.

And the years rolled by so quickly. We enjoyed so many good times, so many of our dreams came true.

Five years into their marriage, the Palmers built a Cape Cod home, designed by Jim himself. He had completed all the blueprints, including foundation, wiring, plumbing, structural, exterior, elevations and floorplans, working on them in the evenings, making practical use of his degree in Industrial Education and Technology and drafting and fulfilling a longtime dream for both of them.

The house was exactly as Pat had envisioned in her fairytale childhood fantasies, complete with dormers, yellow shutters, and a curved walkway lined with tulips leading to their front door.

Together, they had planned the details for the interior: five-panel wood doors, chandeliers, an open stairway, and sleeping areas for parents and children. It was not an elaborate home, but warm and cozy, with love seemingly radiating from the walls.

And then more children were welcomed into the world. Matt was a year old when they moved into their new home, and it was a welcome change from the cramped space in their mobile home. After that, it seemed that every three years they added another son to their family. It would be less than honest *not* to admit that both of them had dearly hoped for a daughter, but in later years, it was impossible to imagine life any other way than with four wonderful sons. They always had been blessing.

On the whole, Jim and Pat's sons were easy to raise; there were no learning disabilities, no emotional disorders, no serious behavioral problems—not even a broken bone until Kevin was nearly through high school. They were each responsible, dependable, well-behaved young children, and they were each unique individuals held together by a common bond of love.

Their school secretary once commented that "you can sure tell that those boys are loved," and Pat had found it to be an interesting comment. What, she wondered, did someone notice about their sons that prompted that comment? And how sad that 'being loved' would stand out as unusual! Isn't that what every child should have?

So, what made our marriage and life together 'extraordinary?' What prompted my quiet mother to describe us as "the happiest family you have ever seen?" Was it the getaway weekends Jim planned so he could spend time with just me? Was it surprising each other with gifts like flowers or jewelry or a special tool for an engineer's design table? Was it small love notes tucked in lunch bags and dresser drawers? Was it praise and adoration expressed so freely to each another? Was it the sheer joy of coming together at the end of each work day? Could it have been the look of love for one another that was so noticeable in our eyes? Or perhaps telling each other frequently how lucky we felt to be married to each other?

Years later, a line from one of Pat's favorite movies would sum it up perfectly: " . . . it was a million tiny little things that, when you added them all up, they meant we were supposed to be together . . . "

As always in the irony of life, it wasn't the big things. It was the daily love that they shared that made it a truly extraordinary marriage.

Chapter Fifteen
New Year's Eve

As the years passed, Jim and I continued to build our life together, delighting in watching the boys grow up each day and falling into one another's arms each night. Each memory was warm and golden like a perfect summer afternoon, with blossoming tulips and gentle breezes. And then, autumn was suddenly upon us: the air grew crisp and the falling leaves turned orange and red and gold. There was so much to be thankful for as the holiday season of gratitude descended onto our lives in 1986, and Christmas and New Year's, my favorite holidays, were just around the corner. It had been such a good year . . .

"Mommy, can I have a 'not-cooked' cookie?"

Pat looked up from folding laundry and chuckled at four-year-old Kevin's description of his beloved 'no-bake cookies'. Setting the laundry aside, she crossed the room to where he was playing with his truck on the floor and hoisted him into her arms.

"Of course you can," she replied, hugging him tightly to her. "But first, I need to bring a few things down to the new family room. You want to help me?"

Kevin beamed and nodded enthusiastically.

The fall had been particularly exciting for the Palmer family as they were just completing a spacious family room in their basement. It was a perfect addition to the living space in their Cape Cod country home and, with four growing sons now four, seven, ten, and thirteen years of age, the extra room for television, games, and parties would receive lots of use.

A box of books and games in her arms, Pat and Kevin descended the stairs together. Pat's pragmatic side wanted to hurry, knowing how many things she still needed to get done around the house before Jeff, Matt, and Randy arrived home from school within the hour. But Kevin's childlike enthusiasm for the new, nearly-finished room made her catch herself and slow down to enjoy the world through her youngest's eyes.

The room really was beautiful with oak trim around the support posts, and a double oak rail that Jim had added to the stairway as a safety precaution. She patted the rail as if to reassure herself, shuddering at the memory of Matt falling under the original stair rail when he was only two years old. It had been terrifying, but thankfully, he had recovered quickly from his fall on the then-concrete floor. No similar incidents had ever happened again under Pat's watchful eye, but still, the new rail eased her mind some.

The built-in cabinets near the stairway were also made of oak, and family photos were ready to be displayed on the shelves.

"Isn't this a great new room, Kevin?" Pat asked the four-year old as his eyes took in his surroundings all over again.

"I *love* it, Mommy!" Kevin said enthusiastically, spreading his arms out wide and twirling around.

Pat laughed.

"Me, too." she agreed. "What's your favorite part of the room?"

"I like the cubbies—they are kind of like the ones at daycare," he replied, running over to once again inspect the cubbies Pat and Jim had designed to fit in the space under the stairs. They had painted them a dark green, and they would make a great place to store games, books, crayons, puzzles and the boys' Lego blocks.

New carpet had been installed the day before, and Pat noted the soft feel of the neutral beige padding under her feet. A warmth settled around her heart as she smiled and looked around the room again, imagining wonderful times the family would share there.

Every once in a while, in an ordinary life, love gives you a fairytale...

"Well, this will certainly be a good place to put all of your toys and books," she said, focusing her attention back on Kevin. "And you know what? Tomorrow, they are delivering all our furniture. Won't that be fun?"

"Yeah, Mommy," Kevin replied politely, obviously uninterested in mundane things like furniture. "Hey, let's leave a note for Daddy on the chalkboard."

"That's a great idea," Pat said, taking his hand as he led her to a child-sized easel and blackboard sitting in the corner. "What should we write?"

Kevin thought for a moment.

"Let's say, 'We love you.'" he said with a heartfelt sincerity that warmed Pat's heart all over again.

"That's perfect, Kevin," she said. "Daddy has worked very hard on this room, so we want him to know how much we love him. Let's do it now before he gets home."

Pat knelt beside him, placing her hand over Kevin's and carefully helping him trace each letter on the chalkboard until the sentence was complete. Kevin grinned with pride at their work.

"Daddy will love that." he exclaimed excitedly.

Pat pulled her son into a hug.

"Pssst!" she said, recounting a secret family mantra. "I love you forever and three more days!"

Kevin grinned in delight, instantly recognizing his cue.

"Psst! And I love *you* forever and three more days!"

New furniture arrived the next day as scheduled. The sturdy pieces framed with pine boards were softened with cushions in deep reds and greens. It was the first time the couple had ever bought an entire room of new furniture, but Jim and Pat agreed that it was worth it. There was plenty of seating for the entire family with a sofa, loveseat, chair, ottoman, coffee table and cabinet for the television and VCR.

Pat hummed along to the record playing an old Christmas favorite by Nat King Cole. At the moment, the Palmer house was quiet except for the soft music and the ticking of the clock—a little *too* quiet for her taste—but that would soon change. She glanced at the clock and took another sip of hot tea. Jim and the boys would be home at any moment.

The magic of Christmas was just around the corner, and Pat had employed the entire family in decorating their home for the holidays. She relished adding little touches to every corner of the house, including a fresh green wreath hanging on the front door. It was full and perfect against the yellow door, graced with a festive red velvet bow with long streams of fabric hanging down from the top.

Jim and their 'four little elves' had already assembled their Christmas tree. The family tree had been with them since Jim and Pat's second Christmas together. It was a bottle-brush tree, adorned with multi-colored lights, lots of child-made ornaments, and topped with a beautiful Angel. Pat had always been fond of that Angel, sitting atop the tree seemingly keeping watch over their little family.

The tree itself may not have seemed terribly spectacular to some, but what it lacked in elegance was compensated for by the fun the family had in decorating it together. This year, it held a place of honor in the new family room, making it all the more special.

Pat had been so grateful for the weekend and a chance to have time to just be at home with her family. She was also glad for laughter and noise in the house as they spent time decorating together—it was blissfully *normal*. Lately, she had been so busy with work and graduate classes at Michigan State University that she knew she had been irritable. It wasn't like her, and she was glad to be returning to her old self. Decorating for Christmas and being with the men she loved most had certainly helped with that!

Tonight, the five Palmer men had been sent on a mission to find fresh pine boughs for the top of the old upright piano that Pat had refinished years before. Their yard bordered a grove of pine trees owned by Pat's parents. In fact, the trees had been planted years before by her dad and grandpa when Romaine was only a boy himself. The task of finding greens was simple and provided a fun time for her active young boys to explore the woods.

The Christmas carol played on as Pat dreamily stared out the front window at the lightly-falling snow.

The front door flew open, and Jim and four snowy, excited boys burst into the room.

"Mommy!" Kevin exclaimed excitedly. "We found a bunch of sticks for you."

Jeff looked annoyed with his brother for a moment.

"They are *'evergreen boughs,'* Kevin," he corrected him.

Kevin looked genuinely irritated.

"They are *sticks*, aren't they, Daddy?" he insisted.

Jeff opened his mouth to protest as Pat suppressed a grin. Intervening, Jim put one arm around Jeff's shoulder, giving it a squeeze, as he scooped Kevin up with the other arm.

"Well, *whatever* they are," Jim laughed. "They are just what Mommy asked for—at least, I *hope* so. The Palmer men are frozen, and I'd hate to have to go find more!"

Pat laughed, helping the boys hang up snowy coats and mittens.

"No, they are absolutely perfect," she said smiling, surveying the bundles of 'sticks.' "Hot chocolate is all ready for you guys in the kitchen. Help yourself."

The boys bounded into the kitchen, leaving Pat to arrange things in the living room. The boughs were carefully placed around the five red candles held in place by brass candleholders atop the piano. Artificial red berries and a large velvet bow completed the look for the focal point in the living room.

Pat was surveying the finished product when two arms circled around her waist from behind.

"So, what do you think, Angel?" Jim whispered into her hair.

Pat turned to face him, her face just inches from his.

"I think you guys did a great job of finding the *perfect* greens," she replied, caressing his face with her eyes before kissing his lips gently. "*And* there is enough left to decorate the case piece in the family room—after all, we *do* have more places to decorate this year!"

"Oh, boy!" Jim groaned with a laugh, as the boys joined them in the living room, steaming mugs of hot chocolate in hand. "Guys, we are in for it now. Mommy is going into full Christmas mode."

The four boys laughed as Jim made a terrified face in her direction. Pat grinned at him.

"Does this mean it's time to start baking Christmas cookies?" Matt asked hopefully.

"Actually, I think it does!" Pat agreed enthusiastically. "Let's head into the kitchen, Boys. We'll make up some sugar cookies before bedtime."

With their four sons racing to the kitchen, Pat and Jim were left alone for a moment. Jim pulled her into his arms, and she felt her body sink into a breathtaking kiss.

"I love you, Angel," he said, gazing into her eyes with a loving smile and circling his arms around her waist.

She grinned and leaned her head on his chest.

"I love you more," she whispered tenderly.

"Impossible!" he countered, shaking his head.

"*Not* impossible!" Pat responded, kissing his cheek.

"A tie?" he asked, squeezing her hand.

"A tie," she agreed with a nod, pulling his lips into a passionate kiss once more.

The days leading up to Christmas were, as they always are, snapshot-like memories, strung together by a delicate thread of contentedness and happiness. It had all the promise of being the most wonderful Christmas of our lives . . .

A week later, Jim and Pat were headed to Lansing, ready for Christmas shopping. The four boys were spending the day at their Grandma Ida Mae Palmer's. She had been alone for nearly one and half years since Jim's dad had passed away, and she always looked forward to her grandsons spending the day with her. They, in turn, loved being at her house, baking cookies, reading stories, playing cards, playing farm, and just having fun with their warm, loving grandma.

It was the perfect morning to be enjoying the Christmas season. Pending snow clouds shrouded the sun's light, bathing the world in dim gold. The Lansing Mall had been christened with white lights and holly boughs, and even the usually-anxious Christmas shopper crowd seemed to be relaxing into the winter morning, moving in time to soothing Christmas carols playing in each store.

With only a few weeks left until Christmas, Pat and Jim had a list of things they still needed to find for their sons and other members of the family. After a couple of hours spent in Hudson's and Toys-R-Us, the pair found themselves seated in Red Lobster, resting tired feet and savoring seafood bisque and cheesy rolls.

"Mmmm," Jim said, taking a bite. "Randy will be jealous when he finds out that we ate at Red Lobster!"

Pat laughed.

"Poor Randy," she said with an affectionate smile. "But he'll get over it when he sees his new sneakers."

"He definitely gets that love of shoes from you, Angel," Jim chuckled. "We Palmer men are certainly lucky to have you keeping us looking good."

Pat smiled at him, reaching across the table and lacing her

fingers through his.

"Oh look, Honey," she said softly, delight suddenly lighting her eyes. "It's starting to snow."

"The guys will definitely want to go sledding tomorrow," Jim commented, smiling contentedly.

The two sat in silence for a moment before Jim said, "So, who do we still have left to shop for?"

"Well, we still want to get your mom a microwave, right?" Pat asked, running her finger down the list from her purse.

"Yep, that's right," Jim replied. "Let's head to Sears to check on that after we're done eating."

"Sounds good. And while we're there, you can give me your thoughts on their tools," Pat said with a sly grin. "You know, in case Santa needs some ideas . . . "

A few hours later, they were driving home, weary but satisfied that they had finished with their shopping. Pat started a list of what still needed to be done in the next two weeks: send out the family Christmas letter with cards and family photo, prepare for their Sunday School class party at their home, make more cookies and candy, wrap packages, pick-up poinsettia plants for the bay window . . . It might've seemed overwhelming, but Pat relished every moment of preparation for her favorite time of year.

The holiday season continued to fly by with happy, beautiful moments and memories to last a lifetime. Several days later, Pat and Jim found themselves saying goodnight to the thirty friends from their Sunday School class who had helped to christen the new family room with the fun and laughter of their annual Christmas party. They had been a wonderful group of friends to Jim and Pat over the years, always ready to have fun together or just simply be there for each other. The night had been filled with lighthearted holiday fun, complete with gag gifts and lots of ribbing and teasing.

"That was so much fun," Pat said with a contented sigh as they closed the door behind their guests. "I think everyone had a good time, don't you, Honey?"

"Absolutely," Jim said with a laugh. "Things are certainly never dull with them around."

"Well, the guys have their Christmas program at church in the morning," Pat said, circling her arms around Jim's waist and kissing the tip of his nose lightly. "I *think* we have all of their outfits ready to go, don't we, Honey?"

"They will look handsome as ever," Jim reassured her, pulling her into a gentle kiss. "You ready for bed, Angel?"

Pat grinned at the glint in his eye.

"I'll be there in a minute," she said flashing him a grin. "I just want to finish one more thing on my to-do list."

"Don't be too long," Jim said, nuzzling her neck.

Moments later, Pat was quickly finishing the last revisions to her annual Christmas letter before printing them out to enclose with Christmas cards and a family photo. It was an annual tradition that she thoroughly enjoyed.

Rereading it once more, she reflected for a moment with a smile.

It's been a pretty good year . . .

December 1986
Dear Family and Friends,

We send our love and best wishes to all of you for a beautiful Christmas full of love, laughter, and memory-making experiences with your families.

1986 has been a good year at our house . . . and as I realize that I am about three weeks behind schedule for our Christmas preparations . . . I am reminded that this, too, has been another busy year. But I am not sure we really want it any other way! Our four sons are growing up all too quickly, and to bring you up to date: Jeff, 13 (yes, we now have a teenager!), is in seventh grade and his highlights of '86 include regional math competition where he scored as a finalist; involvement in Olympics of the Mind; Junior High Church Camp; getting his first contact lenses, and playing on the 7th grade basketball team. I might add that so far Mom and Pop are surviving having a TEEN in the house very well (tune in next year for an update!)

Matt, 10, is in fourth grade and doing well academically. One of Matt's special times came in April as he captured the first place Bible quiz trophy in the Michigan District. He is also learning to do some cooking and continues to have his Dad's interest in "how things work."

Randy, age 7, is in first grade and is busy learning to read. He enjoys being in school ALL day this year and continues to be our "fashion-conscious" son. Randy's love for clothes may financially force him into opening his own pizza place (his life ambition) at an early age!

Kevin, 4, is unlike our other sons in that he is not at all shy! Kevin loves entertaining (for all you Cosby fans, Kevin does a great "Rudy Dance"). Kevin fills his days with daycare three days each week, Sesame Street and "helping Mommy." He asked for a broom and dustpan for his birthday. Women's lib strikes again!

This past year has been extremely busy for Jim with many hours of work and training for the position he will begin in January as head of engineering at Aircraft Precision Products. The career year ahead promises to be challenging. I am again teaching at CMU and continue to enjoy the experience of working with the University students. Jim and I have both taken graduate courses this past year and will do so again this coming year. Education is truly a life l-o-n-g process!

As a family we enjoyed a visit to Washington D.C. in July, complete with tours of the White House, museums (the boys loved the Air and Space), monuments, and a ride in a taxi, subway, and an airplane. This fall we completed a 20x24 family room in our basement and we are all enjoying the extra space.

So much for our bragging (you will notice we left out any squabbles and rough times). God has been good, and we are thankful for His mercy *and care in our lives. We trust you are also feeling His love, especially as we approach our Savior's birthday.*

God's very best to all of you in 1987!

Merry Christmas
Jim &Pat, Jeff, Matt, Randy, and Kevin

Christmas celebrations and parties continued for the Palmer family. Following church the next day, they joined Pat's family to celebrate Christmas at the farm.

"Now, boys," Pat reminded her sons, as she did each year on the drive to the family party. "When you open a gift you are to act like you love it—even if you have *nineteen* of whatever it is and never wanted *one* of them, make sure you say 'thank you.'"

Jeff laughed from the back seat.

"Mom, you say that same thing every year," he said wryly. "And you always use the number nineteen—so, saying something nineteen times makes everything really official?"

"Well, I just want you to know how important it is to act appreciative and to say thank you," Pat explained, trying to remain firm, stifling the chuckle in her throat.

"We *know*, Mom," Matt said with a grin.

"Yeah," Randy chimed in enthusiastically. "We know *nineteen times*!"

Everyone had fun at the family party, playing games, joking, singing carols and retelling family stories. Pat and Suezell even treated the family to their annual rendition of "Willy Claus," using the vacuum sweeper hose as a microphone.

Two days later, Jim and Pat enjoyed an evening out for Jim's office Christmas party. It was nearly midnight when they arrived home, pausing a moment to kiss on the front porch and giggling like teenagers as Jim unlocked the front door. Immediately lowering their voices so as not to wake the boys, they found the babysitter sleeping on the couch and the house peacefully quiet. Jim helped the sleepy teenager with her coat and left to take her the two miles to her home. Pat started to get ready for bed, but then thought the better of it, deciding instead to be a bit playful with a Christmas surprise for her husband.

Jim returned home a few minutes later, unlocked the front door and stepped into the livingroom. It was completely dark except for the Christmas tree lights.

And there, underneath the tree, was Pat . . . wearing only a necklace and a smile.

"Looks like Santa left me something under the tree," he said, clearing his throat as a twinkle lit his eyes.

"An early Christmas present," Pat replied breathlessly, as the world swirled away into passionate bliss.

Two days later, Jim and Pat awoke to Christmas morning, dawning chilly and snowy and beautiful. Jim rolled, whispering into Pat's ear, "Merry Christmas, Angel."

Her eyes still closed, Pat smiled groggily at the sound and closeness of his voice.

"Merry Christmas, Honey," she sighed blissfully, shifting her body into his arms. "Let's stay right here a little while longer—I don't think the boys are awake yet."

"I think you're right," he replied, stifling a yawn and pulling Pat closer, kissing her ear. "We'll stay in bed until we hear them. Maybe they'll sleep late . . . "

It was, however, only a matter of minutes before they heard Kevin.

"Wake up! Wake up!" his voice echoed excitedly from the upstairs bedrooms where he was rousing his brothers from sleep. "It's Christmas! Let's see what Santa brought!"

The four boys scrambled downstairs to their parents bedroom, piling onto their bed.

"Can we go open presents now?" Kevin said, a pleading look in his eyes.

"You bet we can," Jim said, winking at his wife and scooping Kevin up into his arms to carry him down the stairs to the family room on the lower level.

Soon the six of them were checking their stockings hung on the stairway for treasures from Santa, including books of LifeSavers, socks, and gifts.

Pat's childlike side had emerged the night before, begging Jim to let her open one gift early. He had relented, handing her a festively-wrapped velvet ring box containing a beautiful ring with a red, heart-shaped stone. It was perfect, and she absolutely loved it.

As the gift-opening continued, the boys were equally pleased with their gifts. Kevin was already busy setting up his child-sized drafting table and stool.

"It's just like Daddy's!" he proclaimed excitedly, his eyes shining.

He was also wasting no time using his new keyboard and microphone to entertain the family. Randy was thoroughly enjoying the building tubes that allowed him to construct large carts and other objects, but, as predicted, his favorite gift was the pair of inexpensive red and black hightop athletic shoes.

Matt was busily assembling the miniature wooden horse barn and fence he had discovered in one package. He was also admiring the hiking boots that Santa had left for him under the tree. Jeff, staying true to his hero, Alex P. Keaton from *Family Ties*, was taking great delight in the books, chess set, globe, and Swatch watch that he had received.

Jim donned his new overcoat and hat and posed for a photo.

"I love it. Thank you, Angel." He said, hugging his wife.

"And what did Santa bring you?"

"Oh, he brought me this gorgeous dress—look, it fits perfectly," Pat said as she twirled around in the new black and white striped dress. "And he left me a string of pearls and a very elegant dresser set with this mirror, brush and comb."

"You must have been very good this year," Jim said with a wink.

Pat grinned and blew him a kiss.

The next morning, Pat's eyelids felt heavy as she opened them. She sat up slowly, clearing the cobwebs from her foggy mind and smiling at the memories from the day before. It had truly been a magical Christmas.

Slipping from bed, Pat headed into the kitchen, put some water on for tea and began making breakfast. The rest of the family was still asleep, and she decided to take advantage of the time alone to get a head start on the rest of the day.

It was Jim's 38th birthday, and Pat had always been determined to make certain it was celebrated separately from Christmas. This year, he had requested a carrot cake so Pat began chopping nuts, shredding carrots, and draining pineapple in preparation for the cake.

Twenty minutes later, scrambled eggs were already sizzling in a big frying pan when Jim came in the kitchen, pulling his bathrobe around him and still looking sleepy.

"Happy Birthday, Honey!" Pat said softly, putting her arms around his neck and pulling him into a good morning kiss.

"Mmmm—Good morning, Angel," he replied, smiling warmly into her eyes as he put his arms around her waist. "You should've woken me up sooner—I would've helped with breakfast."

"No way," Pat shook her head, kissing his cheek. "It's your birthday. You sit right down, and I'll get you some coffee."

Jim eased himself into a kitchen chair, watching her pour the hot, dark liquid into a mug and cross the room to him.

He smiled.

"What?" Pat asked, handing the mug to him with a grin.

Jim took the mug, set it on the table and pulled her onto his lap.

"I just think you're beautiful," he replied, nuzzling her face with his nose. "And I'm just sitting here thinking how lucky I am to be married to you."

Pat's eyes softened.

"Oh, Jim," she sighed happily. "You are so sweet, so good to me."

He grinned at her before pulling her lips into a passionate kiss.

The family celebrated Jim's birthday dinner with Jim's mom, Ida Mae. The party was simple, with home-cooked food and homemade cards from the boys and a romantic card from Pat signed, as always, 'Never Ending Love.' Jim was both surprised and pleased with his birthday present, a special lathe tool that he had been wanting, and he immediately began making plans for its use.

Both Jim and Pat had the week between Christmas and New Years off of work. They slept late everyday and spent the rest of the day playing with the boys, visiting Grandma Ida Mae, and enjoying their new Christmas gifts. One morning, enough snow had fallen to make a snowman, an entire morning's project for the five Palmer men.

As New Year's Eve approached, Jim and Pat held a 'family meeting' one evening over dinner, asking their four sons how they wanted to ring in the New Year. There was the party at the church, the possibility of a movie and dinner out, and then Jim had suggested a family party at home with just the six of them. After some discussion, everyone agreed on an evening at home.

New Year's Eve arrived with snow blowing into new drifts in the chilly wind. Pat was busily making homemade pizza with frozen bread dough for the crust, lots of mozzarella cheese, tangy pizza sauce, and their choice of toppings, along with hotdogs cut into thin slices. Snacks for the evening also included cookies, chips, pop, and caramel corn. Pat sighed at the array of high calorie treats, suddenly worrying about all of the food she had eaten during the holidays, but immediately dismissed any thoughts about her diet.

After the holidays, it's back to worrying about that . . . This is a special time, and I'm just going to enjoy it.

From the kitchen, Pat could suddenly hear her sons greeting Jim as he came in the front door.

"Well, guys," Jim was saying as Pat joined them in the livingroom. "I rented a video for us to watch tonight."

"What did you get, Dad?" Randy asked curiously.

"It's called *Short Circuit*," Jim replied, handing the video to Jeff. "I think we will all like this one: I heard it's really good, *and* it means we can use our new VCR."

"Is it about a circuit like you added to the electrical panel in the basement for the new family room?" Jeff asked, studying the movie box closely.

Jim grinned at him and tousled his hair, giving him a brief description of the circuits in the basement.

"I heard that this movie is about a robot, though," he added. "So, we'll have to see if it's the same kind."

Soon, the pizza was hot and fresh from the oven, and the family ate heartily. Later on, they retired to the new family room with large bowls of popcorn and sodas to watch the film. The whole family enjoyed *Short Circuit*, mimicking the main character's line, "No disassemble" for hours afterward.

Next, Jeff and Matt challenged Jim to a few rounds of Connect Four and checkers, while Randy and Kevin joined their mom in making party hats for everyone. By about ten o'clock, it was time for the boys to head off to bed. Jim tucked them in and listened to their prayers before joining his wife in the family room. They did some cleaning up before settling down onto the sofa, cuddling up together.

"Tonight was fun, wasn't it?" Pat reflected happily.

"Yeah, I wish we did this more often," Jim said wishfully. "We always seem to be so busy, but this week has been so great. And I think the boys loved our party."

"Me, too," Pat said with a satisfied smile. "I hate to see this week end, Jim. It's been so nice being all together. Next week, we have to return to the real world, huh?"

"I'm afraid so, Angel," Jim replied.

The two sat in silence for a moment.

"You know, I was thinking this evening about our Christmas letter," Pat commented. "This really has been a good year, hasn't it?"

"It really has been," Jim replied thoughtfully. "The kids are at good ages, out of diapers but still young enough to want to be with us."

"We really are lucky," Pat smiled, snuggling closer to Jim. "Those kids keep making us look good. We are so lucky."

"In so many ways . . . wouldn't it be nice if we could just put time on hold and have these years last longer?" Jim reflected wistfully.

"Yes, it would," Pat said softly, slowly letting the thought sink in. "So, Honey, for us, what do you think the best part of our marriage has been?"

"Oh, Angel," he whispered, tenderly kissing her face. "It has to be *right now*. I mean, it just keeps getting better and better, doesn't it?"

"You're right," she murmured amid his kisses. "This is the *best* time."

The couple lit some candles, turned out the lights, and made love in the family room before going to bed shortly after eleven o'clock—1987 could wait.

CHAPTER SIXTEEN
Winter

But time has a way of marching on, with little regard for the people and joys that feel eternal and frozen . . . Far too often, just when life seems golden, perfect and unshakeable, life throws a curveball that you didn't see coming—an awful twist of fate that you pray is just a terrible, terrible nightmare . . . But it isn't.

It was bleak and cold Monday in late January. Springtime tulips seemed to be a distant memory as drifts of snow and glassy ice were taking root in the world in the weeks since the birth of a new year.

Pat and Jim were once again busy with careers and family. Jim was nearly four weeks into his new position as head of engineering at a small aircraft manufacturing plant, and Pat was in the early weeks of the second semester of teaching interior design and housing courses at Central Michigan University. Both of their professional lives included new aspects, with Pat teaching a new course for the first time, and Jim's recent promotion bringing with it the new challenge of quoting jobs that the factory would design and manufacture for aircraft engines during the next two years. Jim and Pat were, as always, there to listen and encourage one another. True to tradition, each night, Pat would ease herself onto Jim's lap, and they would share their triumphs and challenges of another day's work. Each was proud of the other and anxious to have the other succeed. Life was full of balancing four boys, church activities, careers, and graduate classes. All the pieces of their lives worked so well together making it easy to juggle all the moving parts and find joy in doing so. Life was good.

Every once in a while, in an ordinary life, love gives you a fairytale . . . Then suddenly everything in our world changed . . . forever.

Pat was crossing a street on Central Michigan University's bustling campus, hurrying to teach her next class when suddenly, out of nowhere, brakes squealed, tires skidded on the ice. A car was already careening uncontrollably toward Pat when she realized it was going to hit her.

It seemed to happen in slow motion, and she remembered vaguely being aware that she was in front of Wightman Hall, the place where she'd first met Jim . . .

Please, God! Let me see him again . . .

A few seconds later, there was a sickening crunch as chrome and metal slammed against her hip and side. Pat was lying on the icy pavement as the driver scrambled out of the car. "I'm all right," Pat heard herself saying over and over as students gathered around and someone helped her to her feet. She assured worried bystanders that she was fine, nothing was broken, and she was able to walk. Miraculously, she picked up her course materials scattered around her and proceeded to class, continuing to teach for the next hour until she began to feel the impact of the accident and wonder about what could have resulted internally from a collision like that.

"Hi, Honey," Pat said into the phone. It was shortly before noon, and she had slipped away to her office to call Jim.

"Hi, Angel," his voice sounded bright. "How's your day been?"

Pat proceeded to tell him what had happened.

"Are you sure you're all right?" he said moments later, fear constricting his throat.

"I am," Pat reassured him. "Just a little sore."

"Well, I guess it's a good sign if you're well enough to be calling me," Jim still sounded worried. "Please promise me you'll go home and get some rest this afternoon?"

"I will," she said, smiling affectionately into the receiver.

The line was silent for a moment.

"I love you, Angel," he said quietly, his voice taut with emotion.

"Oh, Honey," she sighed happily into the receiver. "I love you, too. I'll see you at home, okay?"

By the time Jeff, Matt, and Randy's school bus dropped them off that afternoon, Pat had changed into comfortable clothes and was beginning to prepare a large kettle of homemade potato and ham soup for dinner. It was a damp, cold night and the soup, vegetables, warm bread, and apple crisp for dessert would provide a simple dinner for the six of them.

Jeff, Matt, and Randy listened solemnly to the story of the day's events as she used the moment to remind them of the importance of being safe in traffic. They then went about their afternoon routines of raiding the snack drawer, while she inquired about each of their days.

When Pat checked on them later, Jeff was busy reading, as always; Matt, always more hands-on, was continuing work on a Lego creation he had started in the family room. Randy was playing with a Fisher-Price school bus, dropping off the brightly colored little figurines at various stops along his make-believe route.

Pat was waiting at the front door when she saw Jim's car turn into the driveway. He leapt from the car as soon as it stopped and ran to the door, pulling Pat into his arms.

She leaned her head on his chest as she felt his arms tighten around her.

"*Thank God* I still have you to hold!" he whispered into her hair, obviously still shaken and frightened.

Tears sprung to her eyes.

"I really am fine, Honey," she said softly, stroking his face tenderly as he continued to hold her.

"We are so lucky, Angel" he murmured. "I don't know what I'd do if I lost you!"

Pat nodded, still clinging to him.

"We are lucky in so many ways," she agreed, kissing him gently.

Suddenly, Pat laughed as her eye caught movement in the parked car.

"Oh, Honey," she giggled, the emotion and stress of the day slowly melting away. "You better get Kevin."

"Yeah, I kind of left the poor little guy in the car, didn't I?" Jim admitted sheepishly. Moments later, an energetic Kevin bounded through the door full of stories from the day and full of warm hugs for 'Mommy'.

The family gathered around the kitchen table, gave thanks for the food, and began eating. The boys talked about their days, then began asking questions about everything: Matt asking how a sump pump worked to Jeff asking how to calculate the tread depth of the stairway to the basement. Randy beamed as he described how his first grade teacher had let him choose pictures out of the J.C. Penney catalog to illustrate the story he was writing. Kevin interjected, as best as he could with his brothers' conversations going on, about the fort he and his friend, Brian, were building at daycare.

The six of them joked, laughed, and delighted in being together. It was a typical dinner at the Palmer house.

After dinner, the boys left for the family room as Pat curled up on Jim's lap while he finished his coffee. They cuddled, kissed and shared the day's events before reluctantly getting up to clear the table.

"Ow," Pat winced as she struggled to rise.

"That didn't sound good," Jim said, worry coloring his tone once more.

"I guess I'm starting to feel a little sore," Pat said, making a face.

"Why don't you take something for the pain?" Jim suggested, putting his arms around her.

"But the boys—"

"I'll listen to Randy read, and spend some time with the boys," he assured her with a grin. "And they'll probably talk me into a game of Connect Four or Memory. I just want you to take it easy, okay?"

Pat smiled at him.

"Okay, Honey."

"At least tomorrow is your day to work at home," Jim added, reaching into the cupboard for some Tylenol.

"That's true," Pat agreed. "I can't imagine having to teach feeling like this; although, I do have a lot of prep work to do tomorrow. I have to write a test."

Jim handed her two pills and a glass of water.

"That class is more work than you imagined, isn't it, Angel?"
"Yeah, it is," Pat admitted with a sigh. "It's just that it's a pretty steep learning curve for me . . . But it'll get easier, I think . . . I hope."

"Well, just take it easy tonight; I'll take care of the guys. Don't worry about a thing, okay?" Jim assured her, squeezing her hand. An uneventful evening continued. Hours later, Jim tucked the boys in bed, listening to their prayers before returning downstairs to see how Pat was faring.

"Oh, I'm fine, Honey," she said, feeling drained as she peeked over the blankets up at Jim. "I'm a little sore, and I'll probably have quite the black and blue hip tomorrow—but that's all."

"Oh, is that *all*?" Jim teased before turning serious. "I'm just afraid it might bring back that back pain you had last summer during our trip to D.C. Promise me you will call the doctor tomorrow and get it checked out."

"I promise," she said with a sigh. "I will call the doctor tomorrow."

"I just want you to be okay, Angel," he responded, tenderness filling his eyes. "I love you!"

"I love you more" she replied, smiling up at him.

"Impossible" he said, crawling under the blankets and putting his arms around her.

"*Not* impossible," she countered.

"A tie?" he offered, kissing her gently.

"A tie," she agreed.

Jim and Pat's lips met in a kiss and moments later, they were asleep, blissfully safe in each others' arms.

"Good morning, Angel. How are you feeling?" Pat heard Jim whisper in their dimly-lit bedroom the next morning. She opened her eyes to see him standing next to the bed, dressed in his freshly-pressed blue dress shirt and tie, dark navy slacks and comfortable wingtips, a sleepy Kevin in his arms.

"Hi, Honey." she said wearily, kissing the fingers of his outstretched hand. "Feeling a bit achy, but I'll be okay. How are you this morning?"

Jim smiled.

"Just finished my coffee, and I'm ready to head out for work," he said. "Jeff, Randy and Matt are ready and waiting for the bus, and this little guy—" he set Kevin down into Pat's arms—"this little guy wanted Mommy."

Pat pulled the sleepy little boy close to her, tucking the blanket around him as he drifted back to sleep. She turned her attention back to Jim and noticed he had knelt next to the bed and was watching her closely.

"What is it?" she asked, stifling a yawn.

He grinned.

"I'm the luckiest man in the world, that's all," he said, brushing a strand of hair from her forehead and gently stroking her face. "Just realizing it all over again watching you two just now."

Pat smiled affectionately at him.

"I love you, Honey," she said softly, staring into his eyes. "Have a wonderful day, okay?"

Jim leaned over and tenderly kissed her lips.

"Angel," he whispered, his face still inches from hers. "I love you, too."

Pat and Kevin finally emerged from bed a couple of hours later, heading into the kitchen for Cheerios, toast and fruit juice. Pat took a package of pork chops out of the freezer to thaw for dinner as Kevin settled on the floor in the family room to watch his beloved *Sesame Street* on CMU Public Television. Pat called to schedule a doctor's appointment for her aching back and hip before settling into her work, comfortably sitting cross-legged on her bed.

The phone rang just before ten a.m., and Pat smiled, certain it was Jim calling to check on her. She almost answered it, "Hi, Honey," but thought the better of it, saying 'Hello?' instead.

It wasn't Jim on the phone.

"Pat?" a woman's voice said.

"Yes?" Pat replied uncertainly, unsure who she was talking to.

"This is Laura from Aircraft." Pat immediately recognized the name of the young blonde receptionist from Jim's plant.

"Hi, Laura," Pat said brightly. "What can I do for you?"

The girl sounded small and frightened.

"Pat, Jim has collapsed, and they are taking him to hospital," Laura said, her voice trembling with emotion. "You need to call someone and have them take you to the hospital right away."

In that moment, I felt the world swirling away . . . spiraling completely out of control . . .

"What's happened?" Pat asked, instantly frantic. "Laura, *what's wrong with him*?!"

"We don't know," Laura replied, tears in her voice. "But he isn't breathing on his own. Please, Pat. You need to call someone, and go to the hospital."

"I can drive myself," Pat said, wondering if Laura didn't realize that the family had two cars. Calling someone would only waste precious time.

I must get to Jim . . . !

"NO, Pat," Laura insisted forcefully. "You need to call someone."

This must be serious . . .

Pat hung up the phone and called her sister-in-law, before rushing to get Kevin dressed and throwing on the clothes she had worn the day before.

Pat dialed the Plant again.

"Laura, what's happening? How is he?"

"Pat, we are doing what we can. They are giving him CPR—you need to keep the phone lines clear," Laura said, obviously fearful.

"Okay, but start a prayer chain, please?" Pat pleaded, trying to stay calm. "Ask Ken—he'll know who to call."

"Okay, I will," Laura promised. "Now just go to the hospital. They are taking him there by ambulance now."

Darlene arrived after what seemed hours, and Pat tugged hard on Kevin's arm as she rushed him to the car and jumped in.

"We need to get to the hospital," Pat said urgently, buckling her seatbelt.

"What's wrong?" Darlene asked, confusion clouding her face.

"He's not breathing!" Pat said, panic bringing her terror to new heights as the realization of what that meant sank in.

"*Who's* not breathing?"

"JIM!"

Pat tried to take deep breaths, turning inwardly to prayer as tears streamed down her face. "Jesus, *please* just let him live! Jesus, please just let Jim *live!*"

God, please don't take away the most precious gift you've ever given me . . .

Moments later, Pat was running through the hospital emergency room doors. The Palmer family doctor was waiting for her.

"What's wrong?" she asked, sheer panic piercing her lungs.

"We think it is his heart," the doctor said, the worry on his face hinting at the gravity of the situation.

"Can you operate?" Pat asked, desperately searching his face for a sign of hope.

"No," he replied gravely. "It isn't something for which surgery is an option."

"Will he live?" Pat asked frantically, trying to come to grips with all that was happening around her.

The doctor replied with practiced, measured words.

"We don't know. It doesn't look good. But we haven't given up hope."

Before Pat knew what was happening, she was surrounded by family. Jim's two brothers left to pick up Jeff, Matt, and Randy. Jim's mother had arrived, hysterical with fear. The emergency room staff asked Pat if they could call anyone for her.

"Suezell. Please, please call Suezell."

Jeff, Randy and Matt arrived, fear and confusion in their eyes. Pat found Kevin being kept busy by hospital staff, and she gathered her four sons to kneel in a circle on the floor, praying that Daddy would be okay.

Please, God. Please! I'll do anything . . .

It was only moments later that a nurse took me by the arm, helping me to my feet as she began to lead me down a hallway.

In that awful moment, I knew in my heart that the love of my life, my soulmate, and the father of my children was gone . . . forever. It was as if I had sensed the exact moment of his passing—the moment had left a gaping hole in my heart . . . It was as if a part of my very soul was gone . . .

"He's gone, isn't he?" Pat said, a hollow numbness creeping across her mind.

"Yes," the nurse replied softly. "He is."

I tried to pull away from the nurse's grasp. I just wanted to run away, escape this terrible nightmare—It couldn't be real! This couldn't be happening!

But the nurse held onto my arm tightly as she steered me into a small room. Inside, I saw my pastor, flanked by two doctors. The doctors began explaining that the team had done everything they could to save Jim's life. They were expressing their sorrow at not being able to revive his heart. I vaguely remember the nurse waving smelling salts beneath my nose. I felt lightheaded and prayed once again that this was just a horrible dream . . .

I heard the doctors explaining what had been done: CPR at the plant and by the team in the emergency room. I remember looking at them strangely—why were they telling me this? Of course they did everything they could to save Jim—I knew that. I told them I understood. I sensed that even in the midst of the nightmare the doctors themselves were shaken by the limits of their trade, confronted once again with how fragile life is . . . Perhaps they were thinking about their own wives and children in that moment . . .

It was so unfair . . .

Pat suddenly couldn't breathe and found herself pounding

her palms against her pastor's shoulders.

"Why? Why? Why?" she begged between sobs.

"Pat," Pastor Adams replied, his voice heavy with sorrow. "I don't have any answers. I wish I did."

There were, of course, no answers. There were no answers that would begin to explain the loss of my Jim, the love of my life, the man who would have given anything to spare me and his sons the pain of this loss . . .

I was then escorted back to the room where Jeff, Matt, Randy, and Kevin were waiting. I was kneeling by my sons, trying to assure them that everything would be okay when Matt asked, "What's happened?"

They didn't know.

They hadn't understood the message silently conveyed when the nurse had led me away moments before. My four children were left confused and frightened, and, in that moment, I, Pat Oswald Palmer, had to utter the most painful words of my life . . .

"I am so sorry. Daddy had a heart attack, and he didn't make it . . . he died."

"Oh, Pat!"

Pat whirled around to see Suezell's stricken, tear-stained face.

"Sissy," Pat could barely speak as she dissolved into heart-wrenching sobs.

Suezell flew to her sister's arms, and the two held each other as if the world depended upon it.

In that moment, it did . . .

"He's gone," Pat whispered through the tears.

"I know," Suezell said softly.

"I have four sons," Pat murmured, anguish coloring her words. "And he *just* died! *What* am I going to do now?"

Before Suezell could respond, another nurse and doctor arrived, escorting the two sisters down the hall. In a small hospital conference room, a barrage of questions began, each feeling as though she was being pelted with stinging arrows as one person after another inquired, "Do you want to see his body?" "Do you want to donate any organs?" "What funeral home will you be using?"

It was incomprehensible . . . I was supposed to be looking into his eyes over dinner that night—this couldn't be real. I couldn't breathe.

Pat turned to Suezell with grief-stricken, pleading eyes.
"If I could think clearly now, what would I do?"
Pat leaned back in her chair as her younger sister took over.

The fairytale was over.

Frozen raindrops streaked across the windowpane. Pat watched them with a sort of mesmerized indifference, yet was almost irritated by their path of ease from the top of the window to the bottom, traveling along as if they hadn't a care in the world, when in reality, Pat knew that the world was over.
She took a sip of the hot tea in front of her and absently pulled her bathrobe closer around her. So many things needed to be done, so many decisions needed to be made . . . and the boys—the boys needed breakfast. Pat knew there were a lot of things she *should* be doing at that particular moment, but she couldn't seem to rouse herself from her chair by the window.
To leave the chair and begin the day felt like a sort of surrender to the reality in which she suddenly found herself, like she was giving in to certain defeat. To face the coming day meant that the events of the day before weren't all just a bad dream . . .
The day played itself out again and again in her brain, awful memories echoing in her mind: the phone ringing, Laura's fearful pleas to get to the hospital, desperate pleading prayers that God would intervene, the look in the nurse's eye as she led Pat down

the hall to tell her the heartbreaking news, the echoing sobs of four young boys suddenly without a father . . .

"Mom?"

Jeff's voice drew her back to the present; to today, where she sat in her chair, desperately wishing yesterday never existed.

"Mom, did you hear what I said?"

Framed in the light coming from the hallway, Jeff stood, staring at her, concern in is eyes. She hurriedly wiped her eyes and tried to focus on the mug in her hands.

"Morning, Sweetie," she said with what she hoped was a smile. "It's still early; you don't really need to be up yet."

Jeff said nothing, but sat down across from her at the table, his red-rimmed eyes matching her own; it was obvious he'd been crying.

The two of them sat in silence for a few moments, Pat's heart breaking all over again at the pain she knew her son was experiencing, rivaled only by the agony in her own chest. The only sound was the ticking of the kitchen clock until Jeff broke the silence.

"Nothing's ever going to be the same again, is it, Mom?"

It wasn't really a question to which Jeff wanted an answer. Pat knew that. It was a question she'd been asking herself over and over again since yesterday—Awful, awful yesterday—when the world simply ended for all of them.

She felt a new surge of grief; how could she help the wounds in her sons' hearts when the gash in her own was so fresh? Unable to hide her feelings any longer, tears welled up in Pat's eyes and slid down her cheeks. She pulled her young son close to her and felt silent sobs wracking her body. At that moment, it seemed impossible to believe that things would ever be fine again, that anything would ever again bring her joy. Nothing would ever be the same again, that she knew with complete certainty. But looking into Jeff's teary eyes that cold morning she realized that some way, she had to somehow find a way . . .

"Jeff," she said when she finally composed herself. "I want you to listen to me: God is going to take care of us."

"But, Mom—"

"Jeff," Pat interrupted firmly. "I've been incredibly blessed by God. He gave me and Dad to each other fifteen years ago, and I will treasure every single moment—" Her voice broke again and quivered with emotion, but she continued—"God has always taken care of us—*all* of us—and He *always* will . . ."

In that moment, an intense clarity settled around me—one that seemed almost Divinely-inspired: I had to go on. For them. For Jim's sons . . . for my sons! The enormity of that responsibility suddenly weighed heavier on me than ever before. How would I do it all without Jim? How could I possibly go on?

My own words echoed in my head as though God Himself was repeating them back to me. God will take care of us . . . He really will . . .

The freezing rain outside had slowed, and Pat put her arm around Jeff's shoulders as they watched the icy streaks give way to a gentle snowfall.

"Everything's going to be all right, Jeff," she said. "Everything will be fine. I promise."

God, please let that be true! Her heart prayed silently. *Be nearer to me than ever before . . . I need You . . . The days ahead won't be easy . . .*

The next morning arrived gray and bleak, and Pat's eyes felt heavy as she lifted them, dread filling her being at the prospect of the coming day. She hadn't slept at all; she hadn't really wanted to. Struggling to rise from her bed, Pat felt as though she couldn't function within her numb wooden body. Today, there would be more heart-wrenching decisions to make: where Jim would be buried? Which flowers should be placed on the casket? Which casket should be purchased? Who should be pall-bearers, vocalists for the service . . . the message, the obituary . . . the list seemed as endless as their love had promised to be.

Jim is gone . . . It is too awful to be real . . .

Karen, her dear friend, had stopped by the night before. The two had embraced immediately as Pat dissolved into sobs in her arms. She knew that Karen understood the enormity of the ache and loss, having lost her husband to cancer two years before. They had talked and cried in her bedroom for hours, two young widows holding on to one another and sharing the agony of the moment, as well as the worst fears for the moments, months and years ahead. Karen had been a Godsend the night before; Pat knew she wasn't alone.

The day wore on, and Pat was vaguely aware that the house was filled with people: friends from church, colleagues, relatives from near and far. Her dear friend and colleague, Janis, had arrived within hours of Jim's passing. Her parents had flown home from their winter home in Florida and had spent the night, arranging dinner for the boys and holding them tightly as they waded through the enormous loss to all of them.

The Palmer home had been filled with people from midafternoon the day before which Pat found both comforting and a little overwhelming. Food arriving from neighbors and friends was piled high and literally spilling out the door into the garage. January temperatures assured that it would not spoil.

The boys were also kept occupied by aunts and uncles and other family—at least, she *thought* they were. Pat massaged her aching temples, hoping someone was helping them find their way through these dark hours. She, herself, was unable to do more than make certain they had proper clothes ready for the evening visitation and service.

And yet in every moment that seemed too unbearable to

survive, Pat turned to find another friend who had stopped by to express condolences with open arms. Each person a unique gift sent to her by God as Guardian Angels in those dark hours.

Suezell never left Pat's side. She was strong, sorting through every detail of decisions to be made and guiding her sister along in her state of shock. The shock, a blessing in itself, seemed to be her body and mind's way for not allowing all her systems to be overloaded with the enormity of her loss.

The morning was a blur of decisions and nodding numbly. It was mid-day when she caught her father, Romaine, staring at her, concern filling his eyes.

"Pat," he said gently, making no effort to hide his worry. "Have you had anything to eat or drink since yesterday morning?"

"I don't know," Pat answered, vaguely trying to focus as she lowered herself into a kitchen chair. "I guess not."

"You'd really better try to eat or drink something," he urged quietly.

"Okay, whatever," she said distractedly. "I'll try some of the rice dish over there."

A plate of food appeared in front of her.

"How does that taste?" she heard someone ask.

"It is kind of bland," Pat replied, pushing the plate aside. "I can't really taste it."

It was almost time to go to the funeral home for the family's private viewing when Pat found herself staring blankly in the mirror, barely recognizing the woman's reflection before her. Only three short and precious days before, she had stood in front of the same mirror preparing for church.

Two arms had circled around her waist from behind, and she had shivered with pleasure to feel Jim's breath on her neck.

"Hi, Honey." she had smiled at him in the mirror.

Jim had grinned at her and spun her around into his embrace.

"Oh Angel, you just keep getting prettier and prettier."

She had laughed in delight and kissed him.

Pat closed her eyes tightly, willing away the happy memory as tears spilled down her ashen cheeks. Now, the thirty-six year old woman in the mirror appeared as lifeless as a corpse. Her eyes were void of light, and her hair a tangled mess. She hadn't bothered with make-up: it was quickly erased by a wash of tears.

She stared at her reflection a moment more.

Will I ever smile again? Does it really matter if I do? Does anything really matter anymore?

The evening at the funeral home only added to the stabbing agony. The room was quiet except for soft organ music playing, and Pat dragged her eyes toward the casket at the front of the room. Along with her four sons, her parents, Jim's mother and brothers, Ron and Suezell, she approached with sorrow so heavy that it felt as though she was scaling a rugged cliff rather than crossing a carpeted room in the local funeral home.

A moment of panic filled her soul with terror as she stood in front of the casket.

This isn't happening! Wake up, Pat! This is a terrible nightmare! Wake up, for God's sake!

But Pat wasn't dreaming. A fresh wave of tears consumed her. *This is real.*

People around her spoke softly, using appropriate words to say how nice Jim looked and that the flowers of every kind and color were lovely. Pat numbly surveyed the casket spray she vaguely remembered selecting: peach roses, baby's breath and two white tulips that the florist had forced to bloom in January. Draped across the bouquet was a satin ribbon reading "Never Ending Love."

Pat's mind drifted off a moment, bitterly pondering the notion that science had the capability of forcing life into tulips, but not the power to save the life of a healthy thirty-eight year old man.

Life can be so cruel and unfair . . .

"Mommy," a little voice whispered worriedly.

Pat opened her eyes, realizing that Kevin was in her arms and tugging on her shoulder.

"Why is everyone crying?" he asked, confusion marring his little face.

Pat hugged him tightly to her as tears rolled down her cheeks.

"We all miss Daddy," she replied softly, her voice breaking with emotion.

Kevin seemed to think about it for a moment, saying nothing but patting his mother's shoulder, comforting her as only a four-year-old could.

"Kev," Suezell said, reaching out for him. "How would you like to come with me and go read a Berenstein Bears story?"

Kevin nodded happily and leapt into his aunt's arms.

Pat looked around at her other three sons. Jeff was trying so hard to be strong, standing near the door, politely talking with family members who were expressing their sorrow.

Matt's tears flowed freely, though Pat knew that he was trying hard to be a brave like his brother. Randy was sitting by himself in a corner chair, much quieter than usual; Pat sensed that he was truly terrified of all that was happening.

It would be only moments before scores of people arrived at the funeral home. It would be a long evening, and Pat retreated to a side room alone and sat looking out the window watching the snow swirl to the ground in blustery winter gusts. Tears streamed down her face as she wondered if it would ever be anything except winter—would life always be cold, dark, and lifeless from here on in?

Her own words to Jeff the day before echoed in her mind again.

God will take care of us . . . He really will . . .

The smell of wet pine hung in the air. The church was stark and white against an overcast sky and seemed to be framed by the surrounding fields of snow from the farms nearby. I stepped from the car marveling a bit at how numb I was and forced myself to make my way up the sidewalk that led to the church.

Funny that I should remember that walk so vividly. It was one of those moments that I knew without a shadow of a doubt would echo in my mind for the rest of my life. I found myself staring at the steeple, noticing that it seemed to be pointing straight to God. I knew He was present that day, as sure as I knew that my eyes were red-rimmed and that our friends and family were waiting inside to say goodbye to my beloved and lay him to rest.

Please God, I silently prayed, Give me strength . . .

Pat felt too numb to move, sitting rigidly in the front pew of the sanctuary, occasionally absently dabbing at her eyes that seeming to flow with endless tears. She knew the church was full, she knew that her family was sitting nearby . . . She knew that her heart was breaking as the funeral service began.

It was a moment I wished to be anywhere else. Usually being in this church brought me such joy! But, today! Today, all I wanted to do was rewind time, replaying beautiful moments that I had wished would last forever . . .

Dabbing away a fresh flow of tears, Pat drew a deep breath and tried to focus on Pastor Brad's words . . .

"Jim had a passion for his family," he was saying. "You could see that by the way he fixed Kevin's tie just right on Sunday morning; by the way he sat proudly as he watched Jeff and Matt during their Bible Quiz meets; and I remember one night we went and watched Randy play T-ball, and you could see nothing but pride on his dad's face. From hospital visits when Randy was in the hospital, to basketball games, to achievements in school, Jim was proud of his kids. He never said anything negative, he was always positive because he knew the potential that you young men have. And he pushed you to be better, and it was obvious in the way you boys responded to him."

"And . . . " Pastor Brad paused a moment, drawing a deep breath and fighting for control of the emotions welling up within him.

"If you knew Jim very well at all—if you *ever* talked to Jim—you *knew* he had a passion for Pat. He talked about her constantly, he would send her flowers, he took her away for weekends in Grand Rapids and Detroit, and when you watched Jim talk about Pat, you saw that sparkle in his eyes."

"Jim had a passion for Pat. Spending time with Jim made you want to go home and tell your wife how much you love her—he just brought that out in the way he loved his own wife."

The pastor continued as Pat felt her heart break all over again.

"Jim was a good man, a good teacher, a good father, along with being a wonderful husband, and a very dear friend. But the thing I think about most when I think about Jim is that he had a passion for God—he was open to the Lord's leading. He was not so proud that he would not step out of his pew and walk down and bend down and tell the Lord what was going on in his life. He would pray, he would respond, he would cry—but most of all, Jim would obey. Jim was an example of a man who had a whole heart for God."

'A whole heart for God' . . . The words echoed in my mind as the service continued. Jim's heart had always been to me a beautiful picture of love . . . of how love can be pure and powerful, creating transformation in its wake. Jim had such a beautiful heart with a tremendous capacity to love—to love me, our sons, so many people he encountered in his day to

day world. I remember so many people grieving the loss of this dear man, so many lives forever changed . . . and I was no exception . . .

The world in the country cemetery near Shepherd was draped in a gray fog, giving everything the shadowy aura of a nightmare. Pat stood, the boys at her side, perfect stairsteps standing side-by-side in their suits. Pat leaned into her dad, Romaine, with Suezell's arm firmly in place around her shoulder, her strength seemingly the only thing holding Pat upright.

It was a moment she'd been dreading since the nightmare had begun. It was time to say goodbye.

Placing a single tulip on the casket, she paused for a moment before murmuring "Never Ending Love, Angel."

CHAPTER SEVENTEEN
Tulips in Spring

It was a moment of pure agony, realizing that in a few moments, I would have to turn from Jim's grave and walk away. In a few moments, I would have to continue on with life, continue cooking dinner, grocery shopping, and paying bills as if nothing had ever happened . . . It seemed to me to be a cruel reality—for one so brutally crushed to have to continue on, and I was tempted to lie down right where I stood and never rise again.

But I knew I had to stay strong for our sons . . . I was resolved to be strong for them . . . I really was . . .

Then, suddenly my thoughts were pulled to other moments—moments when sheer bliss replaced the empty ache I was feeling at that moment. My mind was suddenly alive with the beautiful moments of our life together, of Jim and me meeting and falling in love . . . so many wonderful, beautiful moments we had been given during a fleeting lifetime . . . How could I not be grateful for so many years of happiness?

And then I was thinking of our wedding day and the request we'd made of God as we said our vows . . .

"Heavenly Father, thank you for the institution of marriage, for creating in us the desire to be in relationship with You and with one another. Thank you for bringing together this man and this woman. We ask your blessing on this sacred union. We acknowledge that you created us to be joined together as soul mates for one another. Marriage was your plan, and with your help we will live together in joy all of our lives."

Pat suddenly found herself jolted back to the present. The past dissolved away as the words being prayed for Kevin and Andrea stirred her heartstrings.

The moment they'd all been waiting for was here at last, and the church was filled with loving friends and family. Sunshine poured through stained glass windows, and Andrea was radiant in a white gown as she slipped her hands into Kevin's. Moments before, she had watched Andrea glide towards the front of the church on her father's arm.

It was a moment of so many emotions for Pat, knowing she was about to watch her youngest son pledge his love to the woman of his dreams, feeling the joy of the moment, wishing Jim was present; knowing that in so many ways, he was . . .

The prayer continued.

" . . . Oh God, grant this husband and wife a great love; a love that is patient and kind. May words of praise for one another flow freely from their lips. May they love each other as Christ loved the Church."

Pat suppressed a quiet gasp, suddenly realizing that it wasn't only the emotions of the moment tugging at her heartstrings . . .

The words of the prayer were as familiar as an old friend, words that Pat knew "by heart" in every sense of the expression. Silent tears streamed down her face as the minister continued.

" . . . All the days of their marriage, may they experience the awesome magic of their love. And when they are grayed and bent with age, may love still radiate from their eyes."

I know this prayer!

The same words had been prayed on this exact day, thirty-four years before. They were the same words she and Jim asked of God on their wedding day. What a beautiful moment, as if distant echoes from the past were smiling down on them all, a perfect example of the simplicity of such moments joining together in time.

"Decades from today, may this couple be found still serving

You and each other. May their walk with You be a testimony to the transforming power of great love. Oh God we ask today that this husband and wife create in their union a living legacy of your greatest gift: love."

I sat there, watching joy radiate from Kevin and Andrea as they exchanged their vows, lost in each other's eyes and anticipating their life ahead. And as I watched, I couldn't help but reflect again on my life with Jim, as I had been for the months leading up to the wedding.

So many memories of love and family and laughter . . . so many moments to be thankful for . . .

Of course, the days after Jim's funeral were numb and cold and lonely . . . I sometimes wondered if I could go on, unsure how to function in a world without him.

So many times, I'd need to make a decision and instinctively turn to ask Jim his advice. So many times, I'd turn to reach for him in the night only to be reminded of the heartache all over again as I found an empty bed where he should've been.

I found myself aching to be held . . . Jim and I were always in one another's arms. I found that I couldn't keep warm at night, no matter how many blankets or flannel nightgowns and socks I wore to bed . . . nothing could warm my cold, cold lonely body . . .

Every day, I was reminded again that the responsibility to raise four sons was mine alone. The boys ached and grieved in their own ways.

I recall Matt worrying.

"We won't have Dad's paychecks anymore, will we?"

When I replied that this was true, my ever-practical son offered, " We could buy fewer cookies, Mom."

I hugged him and promised that we would be okay, and we would still buy all the cookies we wanted.

Later that year, I found Matt sobbing inconsolably one night, and trying to comfort him, said," I know you miss your Dad, but you know we will see him again in Heaven!"

"But, Mom," Matt replied, his eyes filling with new tears, "I am only ten years old, and that's a long, long time before we see him!"

I later learned that Randy worried, too, in his own quiet way, asking my mother who would take care of them if I died. He also asked me if I thought it was something Jim had eaten for breakfast that caused him to die.

Kevin was young enough to keep our hearts tender with the joy of Jim's memory. We all came to rely on his "Remember when Daddy—" stories. They made us smile and cry all at once.

A few days after the funeral, I was crying and missing Jim so desperately. Kevin put his little arms around me and suggested that we "dig him up"—in his mind a simple solution to the ache of loneliness we all felt.

Jeff was very quiet about his grief and tried to be brave as the eldest son . . . looking back, he probably tried too hard to be mature and strong. It was months later when he finally told a counselor that all he wanted to do was run down the stairs and leap into his Dad's arms like he had when he was four years old.

I didn't eat. I didn't sleep. The ache some days was more than I could bear. And nights were the worst: the constant reaching out for Jim in the night, only to find the bed cold . . . my heart breaking all over again each time I could hear muffled sobs in the next room.

But all the while, God was with us . . . Life had, in spite of my own unending doubts, continued on, and here I was, a part of my youngest's wedding day.

I pondered again the words of the wedding prayer: " . . . may this couple be found still serving You and each other. May their walk with You be a testimony to the transforming power of great love."

It was as if the prayer painted a portrait of the life I had shared with Jim right up until our last farewell that tragic cold day. And the beautiful legacy God had given to us was continuing on today . . .

I breathed a silent prayer of gratitude as I was filled with the knowledge that our prayers had been answered . . .

The reception hall was filled with the sounds of big band music and the clamor of a hundred guests enjoying the beef tenderloin and champagne.

Hours earlier, Kevin and Andrea had sealed their vows with a kiss and had been presented to the guests for the first time as a married couple.

The reception was now in full swing, and Pat and the rest of the Palmer family had greeted guests, posed for what seemed a thousand photographs, embraced the newest member of the family, shed tears and laughed out loud.

Pat relaxed in her chair a little, relieved that everything seemed to be going as planned. The food was wonderful, the guests were smiling, the music was perfect—it was promising to be a wonderful evening!

Jim, I hope you can see this . . .

"Mom?" Matt asked from across the table. "Are you all right? You looked far away for a minute."

Pat smiled warmly at him.

"I'm just fine, Matt," she reassured him, her eyes misting a bit. "Just fine."

It was one of those moments she knew she would cherish forever. So many loved ones all there, all together under one roof, celebrating one of life's greatest joys.

Across from her, Matt had slipped away from the head table and sat with his arm draped around Heidi's shoulder. Heidi was beautiful in her bright pink dress, beaming and exchanging banter with Jeff's friends, Andrea and Sarah, sitting nearby. Pat saw contentment on Matt and Heidi's faces; it seemed all they needed in the world was to be near each other.

Pat smiled. How true it was!

Randy, too, had excused himself from the head table as dinner concluded to be near Theresa. The two sat quietly together, a little removed from the rest of the family, with Randy occasionally whispering something in Theresa's ear that prompted a shy smile.

Kevin had not left Andrea's side since the ceremony had ended. He sat now, a grin spread across his face, happily finishing his dinner, often leaning over to kiss his new bride with a mischievous look in his eyes.

Under the table, Pat suddenly felt someone squeeze her hand. Suezell smiled at her.

"It's been a great day, hasn't it?"

"It's good to have everyone here together," Pat agreed, suddenly feeling a familiar ache in her heart.

Suezell squeezed her hand again in understanding.

"I wish he was here, too!" she whispered, tears filling her eyes. Pat's eyes grew misty.

"He *is* here, Suezell," she replied softly. "I know it! He wouldn't miss this for the world . . . "

A hush suddenly settled over the room as Kevin's best man announced that a toast was going to be given by the brother of the groom. Pat watched Jeff rise from his place at the head table and turn to Kevin and Andrea.

"Andrea," he said with conviction. "Your parents, Bill and Teresa, have modeled a marriage of dedication and devotion to one another. They instilled in you and your siblings a respect for the union of marriage and, most importantly, raised you with the capacity to love and be loved."

"Kevin," Jeff continued. "You, too, come from a heritage of love. Our father taught love and devotion by example, through daily modeling the truest meaning of the word 'husband'. Our Mother has shown a tremendous capacity to love and of love's ability to overcome."

Tears flowed down Pat's face as Jeff went on.

"Just south of Shepherd, Michigan, in the southeast corner of the Salt River Cemetery is a grave marker which bears the name of James A. Palmer. On the reverse of that marker, carved in the cold stone, is the phrase, 'God's greatest gift returned to God.'"

"Your union is the purest proof that the phrase is not entirely true. You have shown that God's greatest gift is still with us and lives on everyday in a very real way.

Congratulations to both of you. May God bless you with a great and lasting love!"

The evening flew by all too quickly. Kevin and Andrea looked radiant in each other's arms as they danced their first dance together—but secretly, Pat thought that she and Kevin stole the show with the Mother-Son dance they had been faithfully practicing for months.

Friends gave speeches and toasted to the happiness of the new couple, and everyone danced until Pat was certain her feet would simply give out. There were smiles and laughter as guests joined in the celebration.

Things began to wind down, and friends began to gather their belongings and say their goodbyes. Pat held onto Debbie a few moments longer as they said goodbye, grateful to see the friend who had been a part of her life for so long.

Karen, too, embraced her affectionately.

"See you for lunch next week?" she asked with a wink.

"Wouldn't miss it for the world!" Pat grinned.

The last of the guests drifted away, leaving Pat suddenly feeling very alone.

"Mom, Randy and Theresa are going to ride with us," Matt said, giving her a peck on the cheek. "We'll see you back at the hotel?"

"That sounds great," Pat said with a smile.

Randy put his arms around her, holding her for a moment.

"Love you, Mom," he whispered tenderly.

Her eyes grew misty.

"Love you, too!" she replied softly.

"Okay, okay. It's my turn, Randy!" said a voice from behind them.

Kevin appeared, changed out of his tuxedo and grinning ear to ear.

"Congratulations, Mother-of-the-Groom!"

He threw his arms around Pat, half lifting her from the ground and spinning her around. Pat was breathless and laughing when he finally set her down.

Chuckling and shaking their heads at their brother's antics, Randy and Matt headed outside, leaving Pat and Kevin alone for a moment.

"Well," Kevin said, suddenly looking a little nervous. "Here I go! Off to start my life . . . "

Pat smiled tearfully, words from her own past suddenly echoing in her memory.

"Kevin," she said, taking his hand and squeezing it. "I hope you'll always be as happy as you are today!"

Kevin hugged her again, tenderly this time.

"Thanks again for everything, Mom!" he whispered. "I love you!"

Moments later, Kevin and Andrea drove away, their faces flushed and happy, waving excitedly to the last remaining guests.

It was a poignant moment for Pat Oswald Palmer, watching the two of them begin a new life together, full of the promise of warm breezes and tulips abloom. Yes, there would be many bumps along the way—disappointment, sorrow . . . even heartbreak.

Life is so fragile, she reflected as their taillights disappeared into the warm summer evening.

But life is also such a wonderful, beautiful thing—especially for two people in love.

And in that moment, Pat smiled, knowing life was as it should be.

And it was a good life. It really and truly was . . .

Winter, with its seemingly-endless dark cold night, doesn't last forever, and slowly—ever so slowly—spring begins to reveal itself to you in almost undetectable glimpses that the breeze is growing warmer . . . The lost autumn lingers in your heart with the poignant ache of distant, echoing laughter and vibrant color . . . But spring always returns to you with promise of warmth, unexpected joys, and fresh tulips blooming all around you . . .

I don't know how to describe how we survived it all—me, Jeff, Matt, Randy and Kevin—except to say that God kept His promise: He took care of us. Comforting our broken hearts, easing the burn of painful scars, bringing love into all of our lives in delightfully-unexpected ways. We found peace, hope, and joy in God, our faith, in each other, and in the memory of a truly wonderful man who touched all of our lives and so many lives around him.

In so many ways, Jim was **my** Angel—my guardian Angel—who protected me and guided me down the path of transforming love, helping me become the person I am today: loving me for who I was, inspiring who I could become.

I grew up believing I was ordinary. Just an ordinary, average girl from a small town with average hopes and dreams.

But every once in a while, in an ordinary life, love gives you a fairytale. And this is the story of mine . . . It's funny when things turn out even better than you could've ever wished . . .